RANDOM HOUSE
LARGE PRINT

Everything Inside

Everything Inside

STORIES

EDWIDGE DANTICAT

RANDOM HOUSE LARGE PRINT

Published in the United States of America by Random House Large Print in association with Alfred A. Knopf, a division of Penguin Random House LLC, New York.

Cover photograph by Michael Fitzsimmons/Alamy
Cover design by Carol Devine Carson

The Library of Congress has established a Cataloging-in-Publication record for this title.

ISBN: 978-0-593-16459-4

www.penguinrandomhouse.com/large-print-format-books

FIRST LARGE PRINT EDITION

Printed in the United States of America

10 9 8 7 6 5 4 3 2 1

This Large Print edition published in accord with the standards of the N.A.V.H.

FOR JONATHAN AND JOANNE

Being born is the first exile.
To walk the earth
is an eternal diaspora.

CINDY JIMÉNEZ-VERA

We love because it's the only true
adventure.

NIKKI GIOVANNI

Contents

Dosas

Elsie was with Gaspard, her live-in renal-failure patient, when her ex-husband called to inform her that his girlfriend, Olivia, had been kidnapped in Port-au-Prince. Elsie had just fed Gaspard some cabbage soup when her cell phone rang. Gaspard was lying in bed, his head carefully propped on two pillows, his bloated and pitted face angled toward the bedroom skylight, which allowed him a slanted view of a giant coconut palm that for years had been leaning over the lakeside house in Gaspard's single-family development.

Elsie pressed the phone between her left ear and shoulder and used her right hand to wipe a lingering piece of cabbage from Gaspard's chin. Waving both hands as though conducting an orchestra, Gaspard signaled to her not to leave the room while motioning for her to carry on with her conversation. Turning her attention from Gaspard to the phone, Elsie moved it closer to her lips and asked, "Ki lè?"

"This morning." Sounding hoarse and exhausted, Blaise, the ex-husband, jumbled his words. His usual singsong tone, which Elsie attributed to his actually being a singer, was gone. It was replaced by a nearly inaudible whisper. "She was leaving her mother's house," he continued. "Two men grabbed her, pushed her into a car, and drove off."

Elsie could imagine Blaise sitting, or standing, just as she was, with his cell phone trapped between his long neck and narrow shoulders, while he used his hands to pick at his fingernails. Clean fingernails were one of his many obsessions. Dirty fingers drove him crazy, she'd reasoned, because, having trained as a mechanic in Haiti, he barely missed having his slender guitar-playing fingers being dirty all his life.

"You didn't go to Haiti with her?" Elsie asked.

"You're right," he answered, drawing what Elsie heard as an endless breath. "I should have been with her."

Elsie's patient's eyes wandered down from the ceiling, where the blooming palm had sprinkled the skylight glass with a handful of brown seeds.

Gaspard had been pretending not to hear, but was now looking directly at her. Restlessly shifting his weight from one side of the bed to the next, he paused now and then to catch his breath.

Gaspard had turned sixty-five that day and before his lunch had requested a bottle of Champagne from his daughter—Champagne that he shouldn't be having, but for which he'd pleaded so much that his daughter had given in, on the condition that he would only take a few sips. The daughter, Mona, who was a decade younger than Elsie's thirty-six years, had come from New York to visit her father in Miami Lakes. She'd gone out to procure the Champagne and now she was back.

"Elsie, I need you to hang up," Mona said as she walked into the room and laid out three crystal Champagne flutes on a folding table by the bed.

"Call me soon," Elsie told Blaise.

After she hung up, Elsie moved closer to the sick man's spindly daughter. They were about the same height and size, but Elsie felt that she could be Mona's mother. This was perhaps due to her many years of taking care of others. She was a nurse's assistant, though no nurse was present on this particular job. She was there to keep Gaspard safe and comfortable, recording vital signs, feeding and grooming him, doing some light housework, and overall keeping him company between his twice-weekly dialysis sessions, until he decided whether or not he would accept his daughter's offer of one of her kidneys. Mona had been approved as a donor, but Gaspard had still not made up his mind.

Mona poured the Champagne, and Elsie watched her closely as she handed a Champagne flute to her father.

"À la vie," Mona said, toasting her father. "To life."

That afternoon, Blaise called back to tell Elsie that Olivia's mother had heard from the kidnappers. The mother had asked to speak to Olivia, but her captors refused to put her on the phone.

"They want fifty thousand." Blaise spoke in such a rapid nasal voice that Elsie had to ask him to repeat the figure.

"American?" she asked, just to be sure.

She imagined him nodding his egg-shaped head up and down as he answered "Wi."

"Of course, her mother doesn't have it," Blaise said. "These are not rich people. Everyone says we should negotiate. Can maybe get it down to ten. I'm trying to borrow it."

She wished he meant ten dollars, which would have made things easier. Ten dollars and her old friend and rival would be free. Her ex-husband would stop calling her at work. But, of course, he meant ten thousand American dollars.

"Jesus, Marie, Joseph," Elsie mumbled a brief prayer under her breath. "I'm sorry," she told Blaise.

"This is hell." He sounded too calm now. She wasn't surprised by this. Blaise was always subdued by worry. Weeks after he left the konpa band he'd founded and had been the lead singer of, he did nothing but stay home and play his guitar. Then, too, he had been exceedingly calm.

Elsie's former friend Olivia could be appealing. Chestnut colored, with a bushy head of hair that she wore in a gelled bun, Olivia was sort of nice looking. But what Elsie had first noticed about her was her ambition. Olivia was two years younger than Elsie and a lot more outgoing. She liked to touch people either on the arm, back, or shoulder while talking to them, whether they were patients, doctors, nurses, or other nurse's aides. No one seemed to mind. Her touch quickly became not just anticipated or welcomed but yearned for. Olivia was one of the most popular certified nurse's assistants at their North Miami agency. Because of her near-perfect mastery of textbook English, she was often assigned the richest and easiest patients.

Elsie and Olivia met at a one-week refresher course for home attendants, and upon completion of the course they had gravitated toward each other. Whenever possible, they'd asked their agency to assign them the same small group homes, where they cared mostly for bedridden elderly patients. At night when their wards were well medicated and asleep, they'd stay up and gossip in hushed tones, judging and condemning their patients' children and grandchildren, whose images were framed near bottles of medicine on bedside tables but whose voices they rarely heard on the phone and whose faces they hardly ever saw in person.

The next morning, Elsie helped Gaspard change out of his pajamas into the gray sweats he wore during the day. Elsie wished he would let her help him attempt a walk around the manicured grounds of his development or even let her take him for a ride in his wheelchair, but he much preferred to stay at home, in bed. Just as he had every morning for the last few days, he whispered, "Elsie, my flower, I think I'm at the end."

Compared with some mornings, when Gaspard would stop to rest even while gargling, he was relatively stable. His face was swelling up, though, blending his features in a way that made his head look like a baby's.

"Where's Nana?" he asked, using his nickname for his daughter.

Mona was sleeping in her old bedroom, whose walls were covered with posters of no-longer-popular, or long-dead, singers and actors. Elsie knew little about her except that she was living in New York, where she worked for a beauty company, designing labels for soaps, skin creams, and lotions that filled every shelf of every cabinet of each of the three bathrooms in her father's house. Mona was unmarried and had no children and had been a beauty queen at some point, judging from the pictures around the house in which she was wearing sequined gowns and bikinis with sashes across her chest. In one of those pictures, she was Miss Haiti-America, whatever that was.

Gaspard had told Elsie that some years ago,

his wife, Mona's mother, had divorced him and moved to Canada, where she had relatives. Gaspard had shared this with her, she suspected, to explain why there was no wife to help take care of him. He would often add, when his daughter showed up on Friday nights and left on Sunday afternoons, that Mona also had to visit her mother on some of the weekends she wasn't with him.

"I don't want you to think Nana's deserting me, like a lot of children forget their parents here," he said.

"She's here now, Mesye Gaspard," Elsie had said. "That's what counts."

Aside from his daughter, he hated having visitors. He minced no words in telling the people who called him, especially the clients and other accountants he'd worked with for years at his tax-preparation/multiservice business, that he wanted none of them to see him the way he was.

Mona usually walked to Gaspard's room as soon as she woke up. In order to avoid tiring him, they didn't speak much, but for the better part of the morning, she would either be reading a book or texting on her phone.

. . .

Blaise called once more, around one o'clock that afternoon, just as Elsie was preparing a palm-hearts-and-avocado salad that Gaspard had requested. His wife used to prepare it for him, and he wished to share the dish with his daughter, who this time was spending the entire week with him.

"I think they hurt her, Elsie," Blaise was saying. His speech was garbled and slow, as though he'd just woken up from a deep sleep.

"Why do you think that?" Elsie asked. Her thumb accidentally slipped across the blade of the knife she was using to slice the palm hearts. She squeezed the edge of the cut with her teeth, the sweet taste of her own blood lingering on her tongue.

"I don't know," he said, "but I can feel it. You know she won't give in just like that. She'll fight."

The night Olivia and Blaise met, Elsie had taken her to see Blaise's band, Kajou, play at Dédé's Night Club in Little Haiti. The place was owned by Luca Dédé, who, like Blaise, was from the northern Haitian town of Limbé. Luca Dédé, a better-off childhood friend of Blaise's, had gotten Blaise a visa to tour Haitian clubs around the United States. The gigs had not worked out, and Blaise's career never quite took off, making it necessary for him to work the occasional under-the-table job during the day.

That night, Elsie wore a plain white blouse with a modest knee-length black skirt, as though she were going to an office. Olivia wore a green-sequined cocktail dress that she'd bought in a thrift shop.

"It was the most soirée thing they had," Olivia said when Elsie met her at the entrance.

Dédé's was not a soirée-type place but a community watering hole with exposed-brick walls and old black leather booths surrounding the tables scattered in front of the low stage, which was sometimes also used as a dance floor.

"They didn't have one, but I wanted a red dress for tonight," Olivia added. "I wanted fire. I wanted blood."

"You need a man," Elsie said.

"Correct," Olivia said, tilting forward on five-inch heels to plant a kiss on Elsie's cheek. It was the first time Olivia had greeted her with a kiss, rather than one of her usual intimate-feeling touches. They were out to have fun, away from their ordinary cage of sickness and death.

Several men gawked at them that night,

including Luca Dédé, who kept stroking the thick ropy strands of his beard as if to calm his nerves. Dédé had just begun graying in one tuft near his forehead, which kept catching Elsie's attention. She also realized that he wore the same thing nearly every time she saw him, a white shirt and khaki shorts.

Minding the bar as usual, Dédé sent winks and drinks their way until it was clear that Olivia had no interest in him. Olivia danced with every man who trotted over to their table and held out a hand to her. Several rum punches later, Olivia got up between sets, and on a dare from Elsie, Olivia went up on the stage, stood next to Blaise, and sang, in a surprisingly pitch-perfect voice, the Haitian national anthem. Olivia received a standing ovation. The crowd whistled and hooted, and Elsie couldn't help notice that her husband was among those cheering the loudest.

"I'll put her in the band," he hollered into the microphone once Olivia handed it back to him.

"Make her lead singer," Dédé called out from the bar. "She sings better than you, my friend."

Elsie and Blaise had met more quietly at Dédé's five years before. Elsie had walked into

Dédé's with an old friend from Haiti, the head of the nurse's aide agency who had helped her get her visa to the United States, mentored her through her qualifying exams, hired her, and put her up until she could afford to live on her own.

The first time Elsie heard Blaise sing with Kajou, she was not impressed. Thrashing his long and limber body around the stage while wearing one of the guayabera shirts and loose-fitting pants he favored, Blaise kept singing, along with his band, the same bubbly-type songs and urging everyone to raise their hands up in the air. He would later tell her that it was her look of indifference, and even disdain, that had drawn him to her.

"You seemed like the only woman in the room I couldn't win over," he said while sliding into the empty chair next to her at Dédé's. He never passed up a challenge.

"I got a couple of loans," Blaise announced when he called yet again a few hours later that day. His voice cracked and he stuttered, and Elsie wondered if he'd been crying.

"I have forty-five hundred," he added. "Do you think they'll accept that?"

"You're going to send the money just like that?" Elsie asked.

"Once I have all the money, I'll bring it myself," he said.

"What if they take you, too?" Elsie's level of concern shocked even her. Selfishly, she wondered who would be called if he were kidnapped. Like her, he didn't have any family in Miami. The closest thing he had was Dédé and the bandmates, who were still angry with him over breaking up the band for reasons he'd refused to discuss with her. Perhaps that's why he'd left her for Olivia. Olivia would have insisted on knowing exactly what happened with the band and why. Olivia might have tried to fix it, so they could keep playing together. Olivia probably believed, just as he did, that he needed all his time for his music, that working as a parking attendant during the day was spiritually razing him.

"How do you know this isn't a plot to trick you out of your money?" Elsie asked.

"Something's wrong," he said. "She'd never go this long without calling me."

Soon after Olivia met Blaise, Olivia would also reach up to kiss his cheeks the way she had

Elsie's. At first Elsie ignored this. But every once in a while, she'd bring it to their attention in a jokey way by saying, "Watch out, sè m, that's my man." From her experience working with the weak and the sick, she'd learned that the disease you ignore is the one that kills you, so she tried her best to have everything out in the open.

Whenever Blaise asked her to invite Olivia to his gigs, she obliged because she enjoyed Olivia's company outside of work. And when he left the band and was no longer singing at Dédé's, the three of them would go out together to shop for groceries or see a movie and even attend Sunday-morning Mass all together at Notre Dame Catholic Church in Little Haiti. They were soon like a trio of siblings, of whom Olivia was the dosa, the last, untwinned, or surplus child.

"I'm sorry I haven't called you in so long." Blaise was now speaking as though they were simply engaged in the dawdling pillow talk Elsie had once so enjoyed during their five-year marriage. "I didn't think you wanted to hear from me."

We haven't talked in over six months, to be exact, she was thinking, but instead said, "That's how it goes with the quick divorce, non?"

She was waiting for him to say something else about Olivia. He was slow at parceling out news. It had taken him months to inform her that he was leaving her for Olivia. It would have been easier to accept had he simply blurted it out one day. Then she wouldn't have spent so much time reviewing every moment the three of them had spent together, wondering whether they'd winked behind her back during Mass or smirked as she lay between them in the grass after their Saturday-afternoon outings to watch him play soccer with Dédé and some of his other friends in Morningside Park.

"Anything new?" she asked, wanting to shorten their talk.

"They called me directly." He swallowed hard. Her ears had grown accustomed to that kind of effortful gulp from working with Gaspard and others. "Vòlè yo." The thieves.

"What did they sound like?" She wanted to know everything he knew so she could form a lucid image in her own mind, a shadow play identical to his.

"They sounded like boys, young men. I wasn't recording," he said, annoyed.

"Did you ask to speak to her?"

"They wouldn't let me," he said.

"Did you insist?"

"Don't you think I would? They're in control, you know."

"I know."

"Doesn't sound like you do."

"I do," she conceded. "But did you tell them you wouldn't send money unless you speak to her? Maybe they don't have her anymore. You said it yourself. She would fight. She could have escaped."

"Don't you think I'd ask to speak to my own woman?" he shouted.

The way he spat this out irritated her. Woman? His own woman? He had never been the kind of man who called any woman his. At least not out loud. Maybe his phantom music career made him believe that any woman could be his. He'd never yelled at her, either. They had rarely fought, both of them keeping their quiet resentments and irritations close to the chest. She hated him for shouting. She hated them both.

"I'm sorry," he said, calming down. "They didn't speak long. They told me to start planning her funeral if I don't send at least ten thousand by tomorrow afternoon."

Just then she heard Gaspard's daughter call out from the other room, "Elsie, can you come here, please?" Mona's voice was laden with the permanent weariness of those who love the seriously ill.

"Call me later," she told Blaise and hung up.

When Elsie got to Gaspard's room, Mona was sitting on the edge of his bed with the same book she'd been reading for a while on her lap. She'd been reading it when Elsie had slipped away with the intention of stacking the dishwasher with the lunch plates, but ended up answering Blaise's call instead.

"Elsie," Mona said as her father pressed his head farther back into the pillows. His fists were clenched in stoic agony, his eyes closed. His face was sweaty, and he seemed to have been coughing. Mona raised the oxygen mask over his nose and turned on the compressor, which had been delivered that morning, and whose whirring sound made it harder for Elsie to hear.

"Elsie, I'm sorry," Mona said to her in Creole. "I'm not here all the time. I don't know how you function normally, but I'm really concerned about how much time you spend on the phone."

Elsie didn't want to explain why she was talking on the phone so much, but quickly decided she had to. Not only because she thought Mona was right, that Gaspard deserved more of her attention, but also because she had no one else to turn to for advice. The one friend she'd always relied on, the one who'd been with her the night she met Blaise, had moved to Atlanta. So she told Gaspard and his daughter why she'd been taking these calls and why the calls were so frequent, except she modified a few crucial details. Because she was still embarrassed by the actual facts, she told them Olivia was her sister and Blaise her brother-in-law.

"I'm sorry, Elsie." Mona immediately softened. Gaspard opened his eyes and held out his hand toward Elsie. Elsie grabbed his fingers the way she did sometimes to help him rise to his feet.

"Do you want to go home?" Gaspard asked in an increasingly raspy voice. "We can get the agency to send someone else."

"I'm not in her head, Papa," Mona said, sounding much younger when she spoke Creole, "but I think working is best. Paying off these types of ransoms can ruin a person financially."

"It's better not to wait," Gaspard said, still trying to catch his breath. "The less time your sister spends with these malfetè, the better off she'll be."

Gaspard turned his face toward his daughter for final approval, and Mona yielded and nodded her reluctant agreement.

"If you want to save your sister," Gaspard said with an even-more-winded voice now, "you may have to give in."

"I have five thousand in the bank," Elsie told Blaise when he called again that afternoon. She actually had sixty-nine hundred, but she couldn't part with all her savings at once, in case another emergency came up either in Haiti or in Miami. He already knew about the five thousand. It was roughly the same amount she had saved when they'd been together. She'd hoped to double her savings but had been unable to after moving from her and Blaise's apartment to a one-room efficiency in North Miami, plus she was sending a monthly allowance to her parents and paying school fees for her younger brother in Les Cayes. But what Blaise had been trying to tell her, and what she had not been understanding until now, was that he needed her money to save Olivia's life.

. . .

Sometimes Elsie was sure she could make out the approximate time Olivia and Blaise began seeing each other without her. Olivia started pairing up with other nurse's assistants for the group-home jobs and turned Elsie down when she asked her to join the usual outings with Elsie and Blaise.

The night Blaise left their apartment for good, Olivia was outside Elsie's first-floor window sitting in the front passenger seat of Blaise's red four-door pickup, which he often used to carry speakers and instruments to his gigs. The pickup was parked under a streetlamp, and for most of the time that Elsie was staring through a crack in her drawn bedroom shades, Olivia's disk-shaped face was flooded in a harsh bright light. At some point Olivia got out of the car, then disappeared behind it, and Elsie suspected that she'd crouched in the shadows to pee before getting back into the seat Elsie had always called the wife seat during a few of their previous outings when she sat in the front and Olivia in the back. Only when the pickup, packed with Blaise's belongings, was pulling away did Olivia look over at the apartment window, where Elsie quickly sank into the darkness.

Sitting on the floor of her nearly empty apartment and seeing the dust that had been hidden
by some of Blaise's things, Elsie spotted, by the
door, a Valentine's Day card she'd given Blaise
the year before. He must have dropped it while
leaving. The card was white and square and was
covered with red hearts. "Best husband ever"
was written in both cursive and capital letters
all over the front of it. Inside Elsie had simply
written "Je t'aime." She had left the card on
Blaise's pillow the morning of Valentine's Day
while he was still asleep. She had a double shift
that day, and he had a solo gig at a private party.
They would not see each other until the next
morning, when he didn't mention the card at
all. The night Blaise left, Elsie rose from beneath the window, picked up the card, and held
it tightly against her chest. She realized then
that she needed to move out of their apartment.
She could not stay there any longer.

As she stood in line at the bank in North Miami,
Elsie reached into her purse and nervously
stroked this card, which she'd kept there since
Blaise left. The teller, a young woman with a
Bajan accent, asked if she was dissatisfied with
their services and whether or not she wanted

to speak to a manager. She said she needed the money urgently.

"Won't you let us write you a check?" the young woman asked.

"I need it in cash," she said.

She was sweating as she handed the fat envelope to the elderly Haitian man behind the glass window at the money transfer place.

"This money is going to end up in Haiti, isn't it?" the old man said. "Are you building something there?"

The money would end up, she hoped, saving Olivia's life. Blaise had told her to wire it rather than bring it to him because he was too busy running around trying to collect funds all over Miami.

She had asked for the morning off to withdraw and wire the money, and when she got back, she found Gaspard on the floor, next to his bed. He had fallen while reaching over to his bedside table for a glass of water. Mona was already at his side, her bottom spiked up in the air, her face pressed against his. Elsie rushed over, and together they pulled Gaspard up by his shoulders and raised him onto the edge of the bed.

They were all panting, Elsie and Mona from

the effort of pulling Gaspard up and Gaspard from having been pulled. Gaspard's panting soon turned into loud chuckles.

"There are many falls before the big one," he said.

"Thank God you got the good rug," Mona said, smiling.

Then, her face growing somber again, she said, "How can I leave you like this, Papa?"

"You can and you will," he said. "You have your life, and I have what's left of mine. I don't want you to have any regrets."

"You need my kidney," she said. "Why don't you accept it?"

Mona reached over and grabbed a glass of water from the side table. She held the back of the glass as he took a few sips, then watched him slowly lower his head onto the pillow. Mona nearly pierced her lips with her teeth while trying to stop them from trembling.

"I know you're having your family problem," she said, straining not to raise her voice as she turned her attention to Elsie. "And I know we told you to go handle your situation, but the point is you weren't here when my father fell out of this bed. I think Papa's right. I'm going to call the agency to ask for someone else."

Gaspard closed his eyes and pushed his head deeper into the pillow. He did not object. Elsie wanted to plead to stay. She liked Gaspard and didn't want him to have to break in someone new. Besides, she now needed to work more than ever. But if they wanted her to leave, she would. She only hoped her dismissal wouldn't cost her other jobs.

"All right," she said quietly. "I understand. I'll wrap things up until you get someone else."

One night after Elsie and Olivia had heard Blaise play as a last-minute replacement at an outdoor festival at Bayfront Park in downtown Miami, they were walking to the parking lot when Olivia announced that she wanted to find a man who was willing to move back to Haiti with her.

"Do you have to love him or can it be anyone?" Elsie had asked.

Olivia's voice slurred after a whole afternoon of beer sipping. "Anyone with money," she said.

"My dear, can one live without love?" Blaise had answered, waxing lyrical in a way Elsie had never heard before, except when he was onstage and chatting up the women in the audience with his public come-ons ("You're looking like a piña colada, baby. Can I have a sip?"). Corny, harmless stuff, often half-comic, at least, that Elsie was accustomed to and that sometimes made her laugh.

"Oh, I can live without love," Olivia had said, "but I can't live without money. I can't live without my country. I'm tired of being in this country. This country makes you do bad things."

Elsie guessed that Olivia was still thinking about one of their revolving shifts, an in-home patient, an eighty-year-old man, whose son, a middle-aged white man, a loan officer at a bank, had in their presence, as they were changing shifts, turned his senile father on his side and slapped the old man's wrinkly bottom with his palm several times.

"See how **you** like it," he said.

Calling her supervisor from her cell phone, Olivia had barely been able to find the words to explain what she'd just seen. After the concert, to distract Olivia from her thoughts of abused patients, and perhaps to distract one another from contemplating losing Olivia, the three of them had returned to Blaise and Elsie's apartment and had wiped off a bottle of five-star Rhum Barbancourt. Sometime in the early morning hours, without anyone's request or guidance, they had fallen into bed together, exchanging jumbled words, lingering kisses, and caresses, whose sources they weren't interested in keeping track of. They were no longer sure what to call themselves. What were they, exactly? A triad? A ménage à trois? No. Dosas. They were dosas. All three of them untwinned, lonely, alone together.

When they woke up near noon the next day, Olivia was gone.

Blaise called again early the following morning. Elsie was still in bed but was preparing to leave Gaspard for good. Gaspard and his daughter were asleep, and aside from the hum of Gaspard's oxygen compressor, the house was quiet.

"I shouldn't have let her go," Blaise whispered before Elsie could say hello.

When Blaise was with the band, he would sometimes go days without sleep in order to rehearse. By the time his gig would come around, he'd be so wired that his voice would sound robotic and mechanical, as though all emotion had been purged from it. He sounded that way now as Elsie tried to keep up with what he was saying.

"We weren't getting along anymore," he

murmured, rapid fire. "We were going to break up. That's why she just picked up and left. And that's why I'm—"

The hallway light came on. Elsie heard the shuffling of feet. A shadow approached on the oak floor. Mona slid Elsie's door open and peeked in, rubbing a clenched fist against her eyes to fully rouse herself.

"Is everything all right?" she asked Elsie.

Elsie nodded.

"I wish I'd begged her not to go," Blaise was saying.

Mona pulled Elsie's door shut behind her and continued toward her father's room down the hall.

"What happened?" Elsie asked. "You sent the money, didn't you? They released her?"

The phone line crackled and Elsie heard several bumps. Was Blaise stomping his feet? Banging his head against a wall? Pounding the phone into his forehead?

"Where is she?" Elsie tried to moderate her voice.

"We had a fight," he said. "Otherwise she wouldn't have gone."

Mona opened Elsie's door and once again pushed her head in.

"Elsie, my father wants to see you when you're done," she said, before leaving again.

"I'm sorry, I have to go," Elsie said. "My patient needs me. But first tell me she's okay."

She didn't want to hear whatever else was coming, but she couldn't hang up.

"We paid the ransom," he said, rushing to get his words out quickly. "But they didn't release her. She's dead."

Elsie walked to the bed and sat down. Taking a deep breath, she moved the phone away from her face and let it rest on her lap.

"Are you there?" Blaise was shouting now. "Can you hear me?"

"Where was she found?" Elsie raised the phone back to her ear.

"She was dumped in front of her mother's house," Blaise said calmly. "In the middle of the night."

Elsie ran her fingers across her cheeks where, the night they'd fallen in bed together, Blaise had kissed her for the last time. That night, it was hard for Elsie to differentiate Olivia's hands from Blaise's on her naked body. But in her drunken haze, it felt perfectly normal, like they'd needed one another too much to restrain themselves. Now the tears were catching her off guard. She lowered her head and buried her eyes in the crook of her elbow.

"But there's something else. You won't believe it," Blaise said now in a frantic gargle of words.

"What?" Elsie said, wishing, not for the first time since he and Olivia had stopped talking to her, that the three of them were once again drunk and in bed together.

"Her mother told me that before she left the house that morning, Olivia wrote her name on the bottoms of her feet."

Elsie could imagine Olivia, her hair just as wild as it had been that night with the three of them, and wild again as she pulled her feet toward her face and scribbled her name on the soles. Olivia had probably anticipated her kidnapping and had seen this as a way of still being identifiable, even if she were beheaded.

"They didn't, did they?" Elsie asked.

"No," Blaise said. "Her mother says her face, **her entire body,** were intact."

He put some emphasis on "her entire body," Elsie realized, because he wanted to signal to her that Olivia had also not been raped. She wondered how he could know that, but did not dare ask. Instead she let out a sigh of relief so loud that Blaise followed with one of his own.

"Her mother's going to bury her in her own family's mausoleum, in their village out north," he added.

"Are you going?" she asked.

"Of course," he said. "Would you—"

She didn't let him finish. Of course she wouldn't go. Even if she wanted to, she couldn't afford the plane ticket. She had already booked a flight to go to Les Cayes in a few months to visit her family, and she'd need to not only bring her family money but also ship them all the extra things they'd asked for, including a small fridge for her parents and a laptop computer for her brother.

Just then the sound briefly cut off.

"It's Haiti," he said. "I have to go."

He hung up just as abruptly as he had re-entered her life.

"Elsie, are you all right?" Gaspard was standing in the doorway. He was breathing loudly as he spread out his arms to grab both sides of the doorframe. His daughter was standing behind him with a portable oxygen tank.

Elsie wasn't sure how long they'd both been standing there, but whatever sounds she'd been unconsciously making, whatever moans, growls, or whimpers had escaped from her, had brought them there. She moved toward them, tightening the belt of her terry-cloth robe around her waist. Grunting, Gaspard looked past her, his eyes wandering around the small room, taking in the plain platform bed and its companion dresser.

"Elsie, my daughter heard you crying." Gaspard's blood-drained lips were trembling as though he were cold, yet he still seemed more concerned about her than himself when he asked, "Is your sister all right?"

Gaspard's body swayed toward his daughter. Mona reached for him, anchoring him with one hand while balancing the portable oxygen tank with the other. Elsie rushed forward, grabbed him, then said, "Please reconsider your decision to release me, Mesye Gaspard. I won't be getting these phone calls anymore."

She was right. Blaise never called her again.

A few days later, after Gaspard had ceded to his daughter's pleas and accepted a kidney from her, Elsie had a weekend off and, with nothing else to do, took the bus to Dédé's on Saturday night, hoping Blaise might be there after returning from Olivia's funeral in Haiti.

It was still early in the evening, so the place

was nearly empty, except for some area college kids whom Dédé allowed to buy drinks without IDs. Dédé was behind the bar. Elsie sat across from him as a waitress shouted orders at him.

"How you holding up?" Dédé asked after the waitress took off with the drinks.

"Working hard," she said, "to get by."

"Still with the old people?" he asked.

"They're not always old," she said. "Sometimes they're young people who've been in car accidents or have cancer."

Eventually they got to Blaise.

It was Blaise's idea for them to get married. After the three-minute city hall ceremony, at which Dédé and Elsie's friend, the head of the nurse's aide agency, were witnesses, Dédé had hosted a lunch for them at the bar.

"You should have married me." Dédé now reached across the bar and playfully stroked Elsie's shoulder. He had never married and, according to Blaise, he never intended to.

"You didn't ask then and you're not asking now," she said.

"What if I'm asking for something else?" He moved his fingers across her clavicle, down to the top button of her blouse, and let his hand linger there for a few seconds. In his unyielding gaze seemed to be some possibility of relief or companionship masked as love.

As pathetic as it seemed, she thought she loved Blaise most when he was onstage. She was seduced by something she didn't even think he was good at. His devotion to his mediocre gifts had melted her heart. Watching other women pine over his lithe and flexible frame, not to mention his piercing glare at different faces in the crowd while he was singing, excited her, too. She was jealous of these other women's abilities to fantasize about him, perhaps imagining that life with him would be one never-ending songfest. But every once in a while, it went beyond that, during ordinary moments like when she watched him cook a salty omelet filled with smoked herring, which they'd eat at the breakfast nook where they ate all their meals. This is when they would most often talk about having a baby. He had easily convinced her to get an apartment together and then to get married, why not a baby, too? She'd thought, though, that the best time to have a child would be after buying a house together, no matter how small.

"Have you heard from him?" Dédé now asked her. She slowly removed his hand from her bra strap.

"Not in a while," she said.

"I hear he's in Haiti for good," Dédé said, winking after her rejection had sunk in. He grabbed a few glasses from under the bar and started wiping the insides with a small white towel. And maybe this was his revenge, or perhaps he had been waiting to tell her, but between putting one glass down and picking up another, he said, "He's living in Haiti with his old band's money and a lot of cash from some fake kidnappings he and your friend Olivia came up with together. I promise you I have people on this. If they ever see them—"

If this were happening to someone else, she would wonder why that person had not fallen over in shock. But she did not faint, either. Instead it was as if some shred of doubt that had been plaguing her, some sliver of suspicion, which had in part led her here, were finally being confirmed.

"So she's alive?" she asked.

"Oh, he told you she was dead?" Dédé said, putting down the glass he was holding.

"She's not dead?" she asked again, just to be sure.

She wanted to laugh but instead she grasped for a few more words. How could she have let herself be fooled, robbed, so easily? How could she have been so naïve, so stupid? Maybe it had something to do with Gaspard being so sick that week and his daughter being there watching. She had been distracted enough to trust someone she once believed she loved. Blaise and Olivia must have trained, or practiced, for weeks to take more and more away from her, to strip her of both her money and her dignity. They must have been convincing to the point that no one could doubt them. They had fooled Dédé, too.

"I guess we're both Boukis," she finally said. "Imbeciles."

"Suckers, idiots," he added, wiping the insides of the glasses harder. "I'd understand if they were starving and couldn't make money any other way, but they decided to become criminals so they could go back to Haiti and live the good life."

"It's not right," she said, though nothing felt right anymore.

They were interrupted by some drink orders from one of the servers. Dédé worked silently filling the orders, then, when he was done, he said, "I promise you. They're not going to enjoy the money they stole from me."

"What are you going to do?" She caught the pleading tone in her voice, and she felt ashamed, as though she were begging for their execution.

"You should do something," he said. "At least he didn't marry me."

"She might have married you," Elsie said.

"Clearly I wasn't her type. Wasn't enough for her. Your husband was."

She was asking herself now why Blaise had married her. There were other women who had a lot more money. She wondered whether he was hoping she would commit a crime, steal one of her richer patients' life savings for him. She was glad Gaspard's daughter was around that week, otherwise Blaise might have possibly talked her into stealing from him.

"What would you do if you went to Haiti and found them?" she asked while considering the possibility herself.

"I'd give them a chance to pay me back first." He grabbed a bottle of white rum from the mirrored table behind him and pushed one of the glasses he'd been cleaning toward her. She demurred at first, waving it away, but then she realized that she wanted to keep talking to him. She also wanted to keep talking about Olivia and Blaise, and he was the only person she could talk to about them right then.

"What would you do to her first?" he asked.

"I'd shave her head," she said. "I'd shave off that head of hair she gelled so much."

"That's all?" he asked, laughing.

After taking a gulp of the rum, she said, "I am trained to help people, but for these two, I'd pound both their heads with a big rock until their brains were liquid, like this drink now in my hand."

"Wouy! That's too much," he said, pouring himself a glass. "Don't ever be mad at me. Okay?"

"What would you do?" she asked him.

"The stuff they do to the terrorists. The stuff with water I saw in a movie the other night. I'd wrap their heads with a sugar sack and pour water in their noses and make them think they're drowning. And I wouldn't do that to just them. I'd get all the other thieves who steal from people like us—"

"The naïve people, the Boukis."

"Again, I'd understand if he was broke or she was starving," he said.

"The more money they have, the greedier

they are," she said, feeling herself drifting away from Blaise and Olivia and slipping into some larger discussion about justice and impunity.

"Your revenge would be better than mine," she said, circling back to Olivia and Blaise. "Those two would suffer a lot more with you."

It was not the first time he had been burned. Once a seemingly pregnant woman had walked into the bar in the middle of the afternoon. She pretended to go into labor, and while he was looking for his cell phone to call an ambulance, she pulled out a gun and forced him to empty the cash register. He was bringing up the robbery now, saying he preferred being confronted face-to-face to being robbed behind his back.

"This situation is not ending the same way," he said, his voice growing louder and the pace at which he was speaking becoming faster. "I'm not turning this one over to the police to just drop. And what police? The Haitian police?"

She was thinking of going to a police station nearby and filing a report, in case Blaise and Olivia ever decided to move back to Miami, but she didn't think it would do much good. Blaise had not held her up at gunpoint. She had willingly given him her money. Still, he hadn't even had the balls to take the money from her hand. He had insisted that she wire it.

"I'm having them caught," Dédé was saying, "for you, for me, and for everyone else they did this to. Even if it's the last thing I do before I die. I'm never letting go of this, and you shouldn't, either."

That would mean hating them for a lifetime and dreaming about some type of revenge every day. She did not want that. She would rather think ahead, though she wasn't sure what lay ahead. She was glad that Gaspard was still alive, that he was not one more person whose final days she had witnessed. She wanted to keep moving, keep working. Alive or dead, neither Blaise nor Olivia would be in her life anymore.

The details. They'd been so good at the details. Whose idea had it been, for example, to tell her that Olivia had written her name on the bottoms of her feet? They might have also told her that Olivia had drawn a cross there, as a symbol that she wanted a Christian burial. That last call, she realized, was to make sure she wasn't coming to the supposed funeral.

Dédé poured her another glass of rum. Then another. And even as the news of Olivia being alive began to sink in, she was surprised that a kind of grief she hadn't lingered on was now actually lifting; that a distant ache in her heart was turning to relief. She wanted to fight that relief. She did not want to welcome, embrace, the reprieve she felt she'd been given in learning that someone she believed to be dead was now alive, as though Olivia had been resurrected after days under the ground.

Tears flowed down her face, tears she couldn't stop. She didn't want them to be tears of joy, but a few of them were. Her homeland seemed safer now. Her parents and brother, whom she'd gone back to speaking to more regularly, appeared to be in less danger from being kidnapped. Yet the tears kept flowing. Tears of anger, too. Of being robbed of money that took years to save, and seeing her dream of owning a house disappear along with the children that she and Blaise would never have. She felt more alone now than before she'd met either Blaise or Olivia, lonelier than when she'd just arrived in this country having only one friend.

Dédé kept his eyes on her. They were filled with more concern than lust. Her tears became moans, then groans, then a new revenge fantasy emerged. She was now wishing that she could annihilate Dédé's place, that she could burn everything down. She reached inside her purse, pulled out the Valentine's Day card she was still carrying, and tore it to pieces. The pieces went up as light as feathers when she threw them in the air, but when they fell, they felt like stones and glass shards pummeling her body.

"I'll take you home," Dédé said, and the next thing she knew she was curled up in a ball in the back seat of his car, the same old black Toyota he had been driving for years. He had somehow managed to obtain her address from her.

"You're living on your own," she heard him say.

"When I'm not with live-ins," she said.

The rest of the time, she was talking to him in her head, but no words came out of her mouth, which was half-full of vomit. Yes, she was living on her own, in a one-room efficiency in North Miami, behind the main house of an elderly Jamaican couple. They often left her notes inviting her to dinner, but she was always working and was barely around. She sensed that the couple was being friendly because they felt sorry for her, since she seemed to have no one. She was resisting becoming friends with them. She no longer wanted to make friends.

When they reached the house, she handed Dédé her keys, and while holding her upright with one hand, he tried to open the efficiency's narrow metallic door. Glued to her door was a plate-sized stop-sign-shaped sticker with the dark silhouette of a man with a bull's-eye in the middle of his chest. Above the outlined head and torso were the words NOTHING INSIDE IS WORTH DYING FOR. On the other side of the door was the same kind of sticker, with the NOTHING scratched out by hand and replaced with EVERYTHING, so that the altered sticker read EVERYTHING INSIDE IS WORTH DYING FOR. Next to that was another black-and-white sticker that read YOU LOOT, WE SHOOT.

She'd found the stickers there when she moved in. Before her, the efficiency had been briefly rented to a young man who became more and more troubled over time, until the couple had to ask him to leave. Or so they told her. They'd wanted to remove the stickers and have the place repainted, but Elsie needed to move in right away and told them not to bother. The words on the door might offer an extra layer of protection from intruders, she'd thought.

Now the stickers seemed to also be proclaiming

some deeper truths. This one room was suddenly her everything. It was her entire world.

"I'm not going to die in there, am I?" Dédé
asked. "No one's waiting in there with a
fizi, right?"

She tried to lift her hands to wave off his
concern, but could not synchronize them in
time. He opened the door and walked in anyway. He was still cradling her as she stumbled
to the bathroom and emptied out her mouth
and stomach in the toilet. When he carried her
to the twin bed across from the door, she felt
as though she were flying, not the good kind
of flight, but the kind where you're tumbling
through the air and are terrified of crashing.

Lying on her side, in her own bed, she slipped
in and out of a fog in which Olivia and Blaise
were waiting, like they'd been waiting the night
they had all slept together. That night, she had
performed acts and said things she could no
longer remember in detail. Had she given them
permission to be together? Maybe that's why
they had abandoned her.

She dug her fingers into her bedsheets and
tried to open her eyes to fight this foggy picture
of the three of them, but particularly of her

telling them to go off and be together, because it was obviously what they wanted. She had become the surplus one.

She felt a damp washcloth land gently on her forehead. Dédé had made her a compress and was whispering comforting words in the air above her head. She couldn't make out most of the words, but after a long pause he said, "You're home."

She nodded in agreement.

"Yes, I'm home," she mumbled.

"Should I stay?" he asked.

Having him stay would calm her down, even if he just sat on the floor across the room and watched her sleep. But then she would still wake up in the morning burdened with her losses.

"You can go," she said, feeling more confident now in her ability to speak.

"You sure?" he asked while stroking her cheeks. His wet finger carved a warm stream into her skin, a stream that was soaking up her whole body.

"I wish I'd met you first," he said, widening the circle he was now drawing with his finger on her face. "I wish I'd seen you first. I wish I'd known you first. I wish I'd loved you first."

"You sound like one of his stupid songs." She

stuttered through the words, not sure whether he would find them funny or insulting.

"Those songs **were** stupid." He chuckled, raising his hands over his mouth as if to suppress a deeper laugh. "The man was ruining a treasured kind of music, and he didn't even realize it. Or he didn't care."

"Why did you tolerate him?" she asked.

"Why did you?" he countered.

"He had his charms," she said. And he did. One of them was how he became very conversational before sex. Foreplay for him was talking. He would ask her to recount her days to him. He would want to hear about her patients, her difficulties with them, her thoughts, her dreams, as if to help him expand or reinvent the person he was making love to.

"I tolerated him because he was my friend," he said. "He was like a brother to me."

"So you still like him a little?" she asked.

"Only people you care about can hurt you like he did us," he said while stroking his now-much-thicker beard. The gray tuft near his forehead had grown wider, too.

"People you love," she said.

She didn't realize that she had these many words left in her, and for Dédé of all people.

He was the one dragging these words out of her. He made her want to speak.

"Why did you help him so much?" she asked.

"We are the same age," he said. "Our fathers were mechanics together in Limbé. I knew he didn't want that kind of life. And now it seems he doesn't want a musician's life anymore."

"He didn't want my kind of life, either," she said.

"At first he did," he said. "Then Olivia came."

But it couldn't have been just Olivia. Maybe there was something about Elsie that wasn't enough. Or something about Blaise that wasn't enough. Maybe Blaise just wanted to go home. Some people just want to go home, no matter what the cost. Some people would do just about anything to go home.

"Can I share some secrets?" he asked.

"Can't take any more secrets," she said.

"A small one," he said.

Big or small, she did not want to hear any more, but she didn't stop him.

"That night when he met you, I wanted to talk to you, too, but I felt shy," he said, then let out a nervous laugh. "Women like musicians. They're more fun."

"You mean more arrogant."

"Blaise got ahead of me and I let him," he said. "I've always regretted that."

She tried to imagine how things might have been different, how she could have been spared the humiliation of losing both her husband and her money, how she might not have wasted all those years of her life with Blaise. But she couldn't envision how she and Dédé would have worked, either. Still, she heard herself say, "Sometimes you take detours to get where you need to go."

He squinted as though trying to better understand. She wanted to clarify, but wasn't sure how to do it. She was thinking of something she'd once heard Gaspard say to his daughter about his and her mother's failed marriage.

There are happy marriages, Gaspard had told his daughter, the kinds that are truly happy, where the people love each other very much and seem to be great friends, but he assured her that it was not the only type of marriage possible. There are also perfectly dispassionate marriages, and sometimes these marriages go on for years, for a whole lifetime, until one or the other spouse dies. But sometimes both happy and unhappy marriages end, and you get a chance to switch things around. And some marriages, in hindsight, just seem like detours, sometimes wonderful detours, you take to get where you need to go.

Elsie realized now that Gaspard might have been telling his daughter that at some point her mother had fallen out of love with him and had come to think of their life together as a detour.

"Hi there," Dédé said, interrupting her thoughts. "Are you falling asleep?"

"I'm here," she said.

"I wasn't sure," he said. "Can I tell you something else?"

"Go ahead," she said. "It feels like confession time anyway."

"One afternoon after we played soccer in the park, I saw Blaise lying in the grass between you and Olivia, and I felt the most jealous I have ever felt in my life. It was clear as daylight. He had you both."

"He didn't have us both," she said, thinking she did not **mean** for him to have them both.

"He had both your hearts," he said.

"This won't happen to me again," she said, wishing she'd never have to think of Blaise or Olivia ever again.

"It may not be him," he said, "but as long as you're breathing you can be hurt."

"Go," she said, "before you start singing, too."

"I need to close up the bar anyway," he said. "But I have to tell you this one more thing and I hope you don't take it badly."

"What?" she asked, feeling the heat from his breath on her eyelids.

"I didn't know you were such a weakling with the rum."

He laughed, this time loud and deep, and his laughter was not just keeping her from crashing but was filling the inside of her head. She tried to laugh, too, but wasn't sure she was. Instead she started unbuttoning her blouse.

"I'm not usually this weak," she said.

"Just tonight?" she asked him.

"Just tonight," he said.

In the Old Days

The call came on a Friday evening as I was lying in bed, grading student essays.

"My husband is dying," the sniffling woman on the other end of the line said. "And his final wish is to spend a few minutes with you."

Once these words were out of the way, the woman's voice grew firmer and she immediately turned to the logistics. "Time is of the essence, of course. We can fly you over on the earliest New York–to–Miami flight possible. We can get you a hotel room near us in Little Haiti. The house is small, but big enough that you could also stay with us if you like."

The woman's husband was my father, but I had never met him. I know only one side of the story: my mother's.

My father left Brooklyn to return to Haiti

during what he'd considered a promising time for the country. A thirty-year father-son dictatorship had ended, and he wanted to use his American education degree to open a school for poor kids in Port-au-Prince. My mother had no desire to return to Haiti after coming to the United States alone when she was twenty-two. My father left, and my mother stayed behind in Brooklyn. When she discovered she was pregnant with me, my mother shipped my father divorce papers. They never saw each other again.

My mother, who first told me that my father abandoned us, recently confessed that she'd failed to inform him of my existence—that is, until she heard that he was sick and dying.

"Was he airlifted?" I asked my father's wife.

"He came on a regular flight from Port-au-Prince," she said. "He was doing much better when we first got here. Will you please come? It would mean the world to us both."

"I'm not sure I can drop everything and come to Miami now," I told my father's wife, even while realizing that I was sounding like a moody teenager. "I have school."

"On the weekend?" she asked.

"On the usual," I answered.

"So you're a student?"

"A teacher like him."

"What do you teach?"

"High school."

"What subject?"

"Books," I said. "I mean English. To newcomers."

"English as a second language?"

"Yes."

At that point, it was obvious that we both wanted this conversation to end.

"Please come see him," she said.

"I don't know," I said.

But I already knew I would.

I didn't jump on the next flight like someone with nothing better to do, like someone who's kind of been waiting for a phone call like this her entire life. Instead I continued grading my students' papers, which ended up not really being essays but fragmented reactions to a piece of literature we had chosen to read. I had given them a choice between the school's limited options—William Golding's **Lord of the Flies** or Albert Camus's **The Stranger**—and being strangers themselves, both to English and to Brooklyn, and also because it was a shorter book, most of them voted for the English translation of **L'Étranger.**

"WHAT?" began one boy's reaction paper. "I don't thank I be so kalm if my moms dyed."

Before the phone rang, I had scribbled "AMEN BROTHER!" in red pencil, in the margin of his single-spaced, handwritten, stream-of-consciousness masterpiece. But after hanging up with my father's wife, I wrote him a long note scolding him for oversimplifying and being careless with his spelling. Then I gave him a C.

"So she got in touch with you," my mother said when I met her at Nadia's, a Haitian restaurant she'd opened a year after I was born and had also named after me. We were sitting at our corner table, which allowed her a view of the entire place, from the customers' entrance, through the bar, to the kitchen. Above our heads were several images painted directly on the walls. The one above our table, the one that marked our spot, was the restaurant's signature painting. It was of a plump brown baby girl swimming in a large bowl of squash soup that seemed to be spilling out of the round bowl, which doubled as a trompe l'oeil frame.

The place was packed because a popular rasin band had a nine o'clock show scheduled at the reception hall next door, and some of the folks going to the show stopped in for dinner first. Usually my mother would be running around between the storeroom and her office, grabbing meat out of the freezer and bottles out of the wine cellar. She'd be acting as maître d', hostess, waitress, or bartender, as needed. But when I told her about the call, she walked me over to our table and told me to sit down.

This corner table had been in my life for as long as I could remember. It was where I'd napped in my stroller, where I learned to color between the lines, where I did my homework and read dozens of books as my mother worked. It was the only spot where she could see me wherever she was in the restaurant, and over the years I grew to love it.

I liked that there was no background music at Nadia's because while sitting at that table I over-heard conversations that surpassed the drama in many of the books I was reading. I witnessed and was sometimes invited to join baptism par-ties, First Communion and wedding lunches, graduation dinners, wakes, and funeral repasts. I heard men and women—and later women and women and men and men—declare their love for each other, even as others confessed nearby that they had fallen out of love. I heard parents explain the birds and the bees to their kids as a girl at another table revealed to her mother and father that she was pregnant or a boy announced to his parents that he had knocked up someone's daughter. These patrons, and the restaurant staff, were my mother's and my only family.

Still, why did people think that they should share the most life-changing news during a meal? Had they been biding their time, waiting for a moment when the other person was sitting in a public place with a mouth full of food and couldn't scream? Every now and then I overheard a woman telling her man that the kid they were raising together was not his biological child. I heard elderly parents inform grown sons and daughters that they were not in their will or that they were disowning them. But I had never heard anyone announce to their twenty-five-year-old daughter, as my mother had the week before, that the father they'd never met, a certain Monsieur Maurice Dejean, was gravely ill and dying.

My mother had always been a fast talker. She often spoke as though she were on her way

somewhere. Even her customers at the restaurant, while offering lavish praise and seeking details about the food, could not get her
to linger in conversation. The only unhurried
thing about her was how carefully she chose her
clothes. She liked clingy sheaths and plunging
necklines, black silk and lace slips, which were
so refined looking that I sometimes borrowed
them and wore them as outdoor clothing. I
was wearing one of those slip dresses when the
call came and decided to wear it to the restaurant, even though it was still early spring and
most people were wearing long sleeves. I always
felt pretty when my mother's patrons compli-
mented her on her beauty, because in the next
breath they would say I looked like her.

My mother had concluded our conversation
the week before by saying, "An old friend told
me he's very sick. I asked my friend to pass on
your number to his wife." And how exactly
did this happen? I wondered. What words did
she use? Did she simply tell the friend, "Oh,
by the way, he has a daughter and here's his
daughter's number"?

It was second nature for my mother to sur-
vey the dining room, her eyes never resting on
one thing for too long, but this time she was

literally itching to get away from me, clawing her elbows with well-manicured fingernails.

"Please go see him," she said as she waved hello to someone walking through the front door.

I tried to imagine the child me, observing this tableau vivant: two nearly identical-looking women sitting with their backs stiffened and attached to fancy cushioned chairs that perhaps they were both hoping had an electric switch that someone might turn on at any time to put them out of their misery. Or was it wrong of me to think of death in a jokey way when the person who might want to turn on that switch—at least my mother's switch—was actually in the process of dying?

One of the waiters brought over two Prestige beers with napkins wrapped around the cold, sweating bottles. Once he put the beers down, my mother motioned with her head for him to step away from the table and leave us alone.

"As I told you last week," my mother said, grabbing her beer, "in the old days, when the dictatorship ended in Haiti, many marriages fell apart here. There was a hard line between those who wanted to stay in America for good and others who wanted to go back and, swa dizan, rebuild the country. Your father was in the group that wanted to go back and I was in the one that wanted to stay."

She put the beer down and covered her face with her hands. When she pulled her hands away, I realized she was crying.

"He still chose a country over me, over us," my mother said, plowing her fingers into her shoulder-length weave to reach her scalp.

"He might have made a different choice if he'd known about me." I was on the verge of yelling, even if it lost my mother business. This is why we were talking out in the dining room and not in her office. She knew that being in public would keep me from screaming or being loud.

"Don't you want to see him?" I asked her.

"I didn't see him live the most important years of his life," she said while rising from our table. "I don't want to go see him die."

After my mother disappeared into the kitchen, I booked a flight on my phone for the next afternoon, then called my father's wife to tell her I was coming.

"This is such wonderful news," she said. "I'll pick you up at the airport in Miami."

My father's wife was not at the airport to pick me up the next afternoon.

"Please take a cab," she said abruptly on the phone, after texting me the address.

I had been to Miami once before, with a bunch of girlfriends for spring break, when I was a junior in college. And it was just as hot and muggy then. We stayed in a hotel in Miami Beach and spent most of our time in the ocean. Miami to me was the beach. Now it would be the place where I would meet my dying father.

The house was in the middle of Little Haiti, on a corner between rusting, deactivated train tracks and a long line of ancient oak trees. A white wall surrounded the property, which had a small metal gate on the side. I rang the bell at the side gate a few times before a buzzer signaled that I could push it open.

Both the yard and the house were smaller than the wall might suggest. A short trail led through a cluster of traveler's palms toward the front door, where my father's wife was waiting. She was wearing a purple caftan that filled up the doorframe when she raised her arms to greet me. On each of her bare feet was a string of cowrie shells and small bells that chimed as she moved toward me. She raised her glasses and rested them on her short Afro, then, looking over my pink yoga pants and matching T-shirt and bursting-at-the-seams handbag, asked, "Is this all you brought?"

The bells kept chiming as I followed her through a dark foyer into the living room. The decor was sparse, with a velvet brown sofa and a matching ottoman and a TV console with no TV, but covered with packages of adult diapers.

My father's wife motioned for me to sit on the sofa while she slid down onto its opposite end.

Looking down at her feet, my father's wife said, "The chimes? You're curious about the chimes. They're so he can hear me, sort of, wherever I am in the house."

Caftan, bells, Afro. So this was the Earth Mother who'd replaced mine.

"I'm sure you have a lot of questions," she said.

"Can I see him?" I asked.

"You can," she said, "but you want to talk to me first, to prepare yourself."

She got up, and the bells came to life again. "We both need a drink," she said. "Wait here."

She disappeared down a narrow hallway leading to the rest of the house. I felt lightheaded. My stomach, empty since the night before— except for the glass of wine I'd had on the plane—was now churning with both hunger and anxiety. The chimes grew faint until I stopped hearing them all together, then they started up again, then stopped, then started again. This was not the type of sound I'd want to hear all day long if I were dying, but that's just me.

When she came back, my father's wife handed me a glass of supersweet lemonade. I gulped it to keep from having to engage in any more conversation. She followed suit, pouring herself a glass from a pitcher she set down on the side table next to me. I poured myself another glass, then heard some whispers in the distance.

"Is there anyone else here?" I asked, looking around.

I imagined my father walking out to greet me and scolding me for staying away too long.

"Yes," she said. "The owners of the house."

After a while, when our silence felt too heavy, I asked, "So where did you two meet?"

"Me and Maurice?"

"Yes, you and Maurice." I said "Maurice" a bit louder, hoping it would force my father to come out, but my own voice was beginning to sound unfamiliar to me. She moved her head closer to mine, squinting as though she were worried about me.

"Maurice and I met through friends in Port-au-Prince." Her voice dragged, and she seemed to be on the verge of tears.

"Are you one of those who returned?"

"I left at ten with my family and returned after practicing criminal law in Boston for twenty years," she said, then stopped to catch her breath. "When the dictatorship ended, I went back to see what I could do. I was working with a group of Haitian American lawyers who were trying to help rebuild the justice system, but between the repressive laws inherited from the French Napoleonic code and those passed down from the dictatorship, our hands were tied. The head of the lawyers' group introduced me to Maurice at my going-away party in Port-au-Prince. I was heading back to Boston, but he convinced me to stay and help him run his school."

Maurice. I was slowly getting used to the name. Maurice who could convince people to change the course of their lives. Maurice with a different last name than mine.

"Do you have children?" I asked her.

"Me and Maurice?"

I nodded, though I meant with someone else.

"No children," she said, "but I left my first husband behind in Boston when I moved to Haiti."

"You have no children that you know of," I said, then let out a cackle loud enough to drown out the sound of her ankle bells.

"You have your father's sense of humor," she said. "I'm afraid you won't get to see that because many things about him have been stripped away."

"How do you mean?" I asked. "Can he talk?"

"You can talk to him if you like," she said. "I still speak to him. I will always speak to him."

She closed her eyes for a moment as if to illustrate how they spoke. Telepathically? In her dreams?

"When did he—you two—get back to the States?" I asked.

"A few weeks ago," she said. "Then his condition worsened. We're lucky some friends let us use this house."

"What exactly is wrong with him?" I asked.

"At this stage, it doesn't matter," she said. "It's irreversible."

At our confession dinner the week before, I had asked my mother what she remembered most about my father.

"His seriousness," she'd told me. "He always meant what he said."

One Maurice serious. One Maurice a comedian. That makes him indeed my father.

"Do you think you made a difference there?" I asked my father's wife. "In Haiti, I mean."

"You mean was it worth leaving so much behind?" She paused for a second to consider this, took a deep breath, then said, "There's still so much work to do."

"Did you two not want to have children together?" I asked to fill the next long silence that followed. I wanted to remind her why I was here, but it seemed that she was only going to let me see my father when she was ready.

" 'Take care of one child or a few hundred, which would you choose?' That's what Maurice used to tell me whenever I mentioned us having a child. Or adopting one."

When she noticed me reaching for the empty glass as if hoping it would magically fill up again, she said, "I'm sorry. I didn't agree with him on that. Or his approach to you. Your mother has done a great job raising you. The children he was helping had no one else but us."

So he knew about me. The bastard knew. And still he'd chosen not to get in touch. He had chosen a country over us, as my mother had said. Because it was nobler to take care of hundreds of children? Who would be taking care of his little orphans now? Mother Earth would probably be going back for them.

"Your mother did her best to keep you a secret," my father's wife said, trying to lessen the blow. "She did not want to be forced to share custody. This was also a factor."

"When did he find out about me?" I felt my teeth grinding as I was speaking. I wanted to leave, to go away without seeing him at all, but I also wanted to see him more than ever.

"When you were a teenager. He felt he had already lost so much time that you would never forgive him."

I was thirsty again, like I had just swallowed a gallon of seawater. My mouth felt dry. Still I managed to say, "Did he really ask for me to come here?"

"He didn't," she said. "I did. He was too far along to know much when I got your information from your mother and Maurice's friend."

"I want to see him now," I heard myself say.

"You will see him," she said.

Her ankle bells sounded as she moved even closer to me. I leaned back, away from her. Then

I remembered something from my C-student's paper. He was angry at me for making him read, but he was angrier with Camus, with Meursault, the stranger, for saying that deep down it didn't matter whether you died at thirty or seventy years old.

He'd closed his paper with "It do matter. Avery sekond kount."

I promised myself I'd raise his grade when I got back.

"Before you see him, come meet some folks," my father's wife said.

I leaned on the ottoman next to the couch for support as I got up. My legs felt like straw. I wobbled behind her down the hallway, which was lined with the house owner's family photographs. We stopped in the kitchen, where two men and three women were sitting around a square table.

My father's wife turned to everyone at the table and said, "This is Maurice's daughter, Nadia. She's visiting from New York."

If they were shocked that Maurice had a daughter, they didn't show it.

"Nadia, these are friends of mine and Maurice's," she said.

One of the friends was a doctor. After waving

hello, the doctor went back to tapping on her phone. We were the youngest people there. She was wearing a sleeveless yellow dress, no doctor's coat or scrubs, but had a stethoscope around her neck.

My father's wife then pointed to the collared minister among the remaining four and said, "Pastor Sorel and his wife are longtime friends."

I gave an extra nod to Pastor Sorel, who got up from his chair so I could sit in it. As he pulled out the chair for me, he said, "This must be a great shock."

"Maurice and Nadia have not spent much time together," my father's wife said.

"Or at all," I said.

I couldn't believe I had been in the house so long and had not seen the man himself.

"Can I see him?" I asked again.

"Have some bread soup," my father's wife said. She poured me a bowl of plain white soup filled with soaked bread, potato chunks, and a few white noodles.

"There's plenty more if you need it," said one of the other women around the table. Something led me to believe that she was Pastor Sorel's wife.

As I slurped my way through the soup, Pastor

Sorel put his hands on my shoulders. All the others, except the doctor, linked hands and bowed their heads.

"Let's pray for Nadia," Pastor Sorel said.

I wondered why they were praying for me and not for my father, but like the soup, the prayer calmed my stomach.

While they were praying, I turned my face toward a low window, where the fluttering shadow of a traveler's palm merged with our reflections in the glass, which was being pierced by the orange rays of a late-afternoon sunset. On the kitchen's walls were more framed pictures of Pastor Sorel and his family. In the pictures, Pastor Sorel was always photographed on the left side of his daughter, the doctor, while the woman who'd possibly made the soup was always on the right. Based on the pictures in the hallway, this seemed to have been their picture-taking pose since the doctor was a toddler to when she began wearing caps and gowns, bridesmaids' dresses, a wedding gown, then eventually her doctor's coat.

"We can go in now," my father's wife told me when I was done with the soup.

As I followed her down the hall, the minister

and his wife began singing a mournful hymn,
a lullaby for the dying.

Shall we gather at the river?
The beautiful, beautiful river.

The room was dimly lit, save for a desk lamp
on a nightstand filled with gauze and ointments
and other medical supplies. There was a hospital bed smack in the middle, and on the side,
against the wall, was a cot covered with an eyelet
embroidered white sheet. The bed was directly
beneath a ceiling fan, which was circulating the
cool air from a stand-alone unit on a side window. I followed my father's wife to the bed.

My mother had no pictures of my father, and
he and Mother Earth were not online either
posting about themselves or raising money like
everybody else, so I had no image to compare
with that skeletal man lying in the hospital bed,
except my own. From the outline of his stiff
pajama-clad body under the thin blanket, I
could see that he was shorter than me, though
the illness might have shrunk him. If there was
any territory for me to claim, it had to be on
his face. I had to find myself in his drawn-out
coppery skin, in the uneven rise of his forehead,

in the tightly sealed eyes, the eyebrows that had nearly disappeared, the deep pockets beneath the hollow cheeks, the clenched jaw and gray fuzz on his chin.

I let my hands travel up the frigid railing of the hospital bed toward my father's face, which when my fingertips grazed it felt just as prickly and haggard as it looked and just as dead. I pressed my palm down on his forehead and it was slippery, like a well-polished mask. I turned to my father's wife for an explanation. She began quietly sobbing. Her sobs reminded me of my mother's tears, even though they were crying over two different men, neither of whom I knew.

"He is gone now," she said. "He is free. We rejoice for his freedom." As she said this, her face became distorted as much with agony as horror. "He died right before your plane landed," she finally admitted.

In her flushed and distressed face, I saw the void my father had left as clearly as if it were a gash, a wound, a scar. I was desperate to feel what she was feeling. I envied it, coveted it.

"Why didn't you tell me sooner?" I asked.

"There's no rush, no emergency," she said. She was composed once again, as though she had not been crying at all. "The doctor will pronounce him dead when you tell her to. Whenever you are ready. He's been out of it for the past day or so, but we were told he could still hear us until the moment he stopped breathing."

So officially, at least on paper, since the doctor had not yet called it, my father was still not dead.

"If you ever have a child of your own," my father's wife said, "at least you can tell your child that you saw your father, even like this."

How would I describe this to my own child if I ever had one? How would I tell it to my mother, who thought that nothing having to do with my father was in the present, that everything involving him was in the past, in the old days?

My father's wife had her own version of the old days. In the old days, she was telling me, conch shells blared for each person who died. In the old days, when a baby was born, the midwife would put the baby on the ground, and it was up to the father to pick up the child and claim it as his own. In the old days, the dead were initially kept at home. Farewell prayers were chanted and mourning dances were performed at their joy-filled wakes. When it was time to take the dead out of the house, they would be carried out, feet first, through the back door, and not the front, so they would know not to return. Their babies and young children would be passed over their coffins so they could shake off their spirits and wouldn't be haunted for the rest of their lives. Then a village elder would pour rum on the grave as a final farewell. In the old days, she said, I would have pronounced my father dead with my bereavement wails to our fellow villagers, both the ones crowding the house and others far beyond.

Looking down at my father's dead face, in which I saw no trace of my own, I wanted to grab him and shake him, force him to wake up and explain to me **his** version of the old days.

"He was a good man, a very good man," my father's wife continued. "I know he would have wanted you to be part of his final rites."

How could he have wanted me to be part of his final rites when he'd been absent from my first?

"Please forgive him," she said. "Please forgive us. There is no rush now. You can take your time here, then our young doctor friend will pronounce him . . ."

My father's wife's voice trailed off, then she walked out of the room, which became brighter when she opened the door allowing some of the hallway light in. I sat down on what must have been her cot, where she must have spent days, and nights, on both a vigil and a death watch. The cold air from the air-conditioning unit hit me, and I shivered. I leaned back and pressed my spine against the eyelet sheet. I wanted to close my eyes, but I couldn't take them off the fan twirling over my head. It reminded me of wanting to put my hands into another type of fan in my mother's restaurant when I was little and seeing if it would really cut my fingers off as my mother had warned me it would. It also reminded me of being hushed by my mother whenever I asked her about my father, until one day, when I was twelve, she blurted that he had left her before I was born and wanted nothing to do with us. This is what kept me from looking for him. This is what made me wish he would die.

Out in the hall, I heard my father's wife and her friends talking. Perhaps they thought they were whispering, but they were not.

Pastor Sorel said, "Surely a simple service would do, then the cremation, just as he'd asked."

"He wants his ashes spread on the school grounds in Port-au-Prince," my father's wife said.

She was speaking about him in the present, as though he were still alive.

Led by Pastor Sorel, they all began singing again, about gathering at a river where angels tread on crystal tides. They sang of laying their burdens down at this river and receiving a hard-earned robe and a crown from God.

Yes, we'll gather at the river,
The beautiful, the beautiful river.

Then, during a still moment when neither prayer nor song could be heard, the doctor asked, "How much longer do you think the daughter will be in there?"

The daughter? She said "the daughter." And the daughter was me. The daughter will be in there for a year and a day when, as in the old days—according to my father's wife—my father's soul will rise from another type of river to be reborn as a shadow, a dream, or a whisper in the wind. The daughter will be in there for a lifetime, for the same amount of time she'd missed with her father. How about the daughter just stay here until the end of time?

But even if the daughter weren't a total stranger, even if my father and I had spent my entire life together, I wouldn't be able to stay in that room much longer. So I got up, leaned over the hospital bed railing, and pressed my lips against my father's cold forehead. I did this because I thought it would have been expected of me. If he had been alive and awake when I'd arrived, this is what I would have done.

My father no longer looked like he was sleeping. A sliver of white was visible through his half-open left eyelid. A veiled world remained hidden behind that small gap, a world I had never been privy to, a world I'd never know. In the old days, coins might have been placed over his eyes to keep me from seeing even this much of the windows to his soul.

It would have been simpler perhaps, and easier, to cry, to want to cry, to mourn things I had no idea I'd lost, to wonder how I would ever be able to live without him.

"Au revoir, Papa," I said, trying out the word "Papa" just this once. I had always wondered what it would be like to call someone Papa. I had even imagined my mother marrying one of the men she had casually dated, just so I could call someone Papa. This would be the first and last time I would ever say the word "Papa" to the man who had actually been my father.

I turned my back on all of this, on him, and started walking toward the door. I kept expecting something to stop me, a hand on my shoulder, a whisper that would reverse, if not my entire life, this one incomplete moment. But my father did not wake up, nor did he come back from the dead to claim me.

Aujourd'hui, papa est mort.
My father died today.

But I had already killed him over and over in my mind. In a robbery, a duel, a terrorist attack, with bullets, grenades, land mines, snakebites, drowning, a drug overdose, in a car crash, train crash, plane crash, volcano eruption, tsunami, lightning strike, earthquake, of natural causes, in his sleep, with a terminal illness. This time I had apparently succeeded. He was dead, truly dead.

The kitchen, where my father's wife and her friends were waiting, was darker than before. The window shades were drawn and the picture frames were covered with black bedsheets.

"His spirit might stop and look in the glass," my father's wife called out to me from the front room. "That would keep him from traveling on."

. . .

I cried only after I went to the bathroom closest to where my dead father lay and called my
mother from there.

"He's gone, isn't he?" she asked as soon as she
picked up.

I nodded as though she were standing across
from me.

"I'm sorry," she said. "For everyone involved."

"He had a wife," I said between sobs. "And
nice friends who loved him."

"And we have each other," she said, which
made me realize that she was feeling neither
guilt nor regret at having severed herself from
her past, except for the food she served in her
restaurant. And me.

"Are you staying for the services?" my
mother asked.

I didn't think I could. I had not seen him
either live or die, so I was at best a well-wisher,
and at worst an intruder. Besides, I had to get
back to work, to **my** kids.

"Come home soon," my mother said.

I told her I would.

My father's wife's ankle bells began chiming
again as I stepped out of the bathroom. They
pealed softly at first, then they tolled as though

she was no longer walking but dancing to the front door.

"He died from a type of cancer where the brain cells start looking like stars," I heard her tell the person, or people, who'd just arrived for the washing of the body, or whatever might come next.

"The calcium in his bones became stardust," she told someone else.

Then from the front room came the scratchy sound of a needle hitting an old vinyl record. Nina Simone's sultry yet sorrow-filled voice came blaring out, wailing for us to take her to the water to be baptized. The sorrow soon turned to joy, and the piano gave way to drums as Nina demanded, pleaded, to be baptized.

I suddenly wanted to hold my father's wife, and to let her hold me in a way that my mother could not. As I began walking toward my father's wife, I felt, with Nina's drums throbbing in my ears, as though I was marching at the head of a king's funeral procession, with an entire village in my wake.

The Port-au-Prince
Marriage Special

❧

They told me, madame, that I'm going to die."

Mélisande had gone to a downtown clinic and had gotten her blood drawn, only to receive a possible death sentence. She'd been coughing for some time, soft and discreet at first, then more and more thunderously, which had led to my removing my eleven-month-old son, Wesley, from her care. Only when she got a fever and became sluggish to the point that she was barely mobile did she finally decide to seek medical help.

She was sobbing as she stood in my bedroom doorway, her body as flat as one of the door-frame beams. She hiked up a flowered silk skirt to wipe the tears from her face. I immediately recognized that skirt as one I'd formerly owned. I had paid sixty dollars for it at a shop in Miami back when I was in graduate school, where I met my husband, Xavier, a fellow Haitian, with whom I run a small hotel, which is also our home, in Port-au-Prince.

"Have you talked to your mother?" I asked Mélisande.

She was twenty-one or twenty-two at most. Her mother, Babette, worked as a cook at our hotel. Mélisande was our son's nanny, and she and Babette shared a maid's room behind the hotel's kitchen.

I didn't trust many people with my son, but it was obvious that Wesley loved her. As soon as I placed Wesley in Mélisande's arms, she probed out of him the loudest laugh he'd ever tried. Perhaps what drew him to her were the same things I found appealing about her: her elfin face, her reedy voice, her slightly hesitant gait, as though she wasn't sure whether or not it was safe to touch the ground.

Xavier thought Mélisande should be in a trade school, learning some other skill when she wasn't taking care of Wesley, but we hadn't forced it or insisted that she go. During her free time, we saw her helping her mother cook. I also watched her joke with our two hotel maids as she sometimes cleaned the conference room and all twelve guest rooms with them. The agreement she had with the maids was that whenever she helped them out, whatever was left behind in the rooms would be split with her.

Sometimes, aside from the tips, they'd find pieces of gold or silver jewelry—mostly single earrings and thin bracelets—that my husband would make every effort to return, but if no one called back or claimed them for a few months, we would allow the maids to sell them to the jeweler down the street, who'd melt them into other pieces to sell to other guests. This was money Mélisande might not be making if she were in school and not working for us, but school might have helped with the future. And now she might have no future.

"Come in and sit down," I told her.

I got up from my bed and walked over to the doorway. I was still in my nightgown. Wesley was in the main hotel building with my husband, who was in his office preparing to receive five college students arriving for spring break. My husband also ran a tourism business from the hotel. Our guided tours' clientele consisted mostly of the foreign-born children of Haitians living abroad. During the day, Xavier took them to visit local landmarks and historical sites. At night, they were hosted by our writer, artist, and musician friends, and even shared a meal with some kids in a nearby orphanage. Another colleague took our guests out of the capital to Jacmel, a coastal town that was once thought of as the Riviera of Haiti, then Gonaïves, where Haiti's independence from France was officially declared in 1804, and to the Citadelle Laferrière, a breathtaking fortress built after independence. Xavier's tourism package was also a kind of recruiting tool. He wanted to encourage these young people to come back and contribute their skills to the country.

Mélisande felt extremely light to my touch—like paper, cloth, or air—as I guided her toward a rocking chair by my bed. She slid down into the chair, where I piled a few cushions around her. Resting my arms on her shoulders, I felt some of the warmth of her lingering fever through her plain white T-shirt.

"What did the doctor say, exactly?" I asked.

"He said," she replied, with her face buried in her hands, "that I have SIDA. AIDS."

I had initially expected pneumonia, a bronchial infection, but not that. When she came home from the doctor, I was prepared to lecture her about not waiting so long the next time to get herself checked out. I thought at most she would need antibiotics.

"Even with the SIDA," I told her, "they have all these drugs. People live for years on them."

This provoked a new flurry of sobs. Her shoulders were bobbing up and down, and I began to panic myself. Wesley. She had touched every part of his body, had washed, had wiped, had kissed and cuddled him. Had they ever accidentally exchanged blood? I wanted to leave her there and run past the pool, through the hibiscus garden, the flamboyant tree clusters, to the other gingerbread house, on the other side of the property, to find my son. As usual, Wesley had woken up earlier than all of us, and my husband had taken him to his office. He was probably playing or crawling under his father's desk as Xavier made his calls.

Mélisande was still sobbing. We'd have to have Wesley tested. And how would I live with myself if he had been infected?

I decided to simply let Mélisande cry. Let her get it out of her system before we tried to come up with some type of solution. A few clinics offered good retroviral treatments. Some were free; others expected you to be part of studies and experiments. The clinic where Mélisande had been tested offered counseling but no long-term treatment.

I should have urged her to go to the doctor when she first began to lose weight. I should have stopped her not-so-secret flirtations with some of the hotel's male guests. The night concierge had told Xavier and me that Mélisande liked to seek out some particular guests for conversations—the fat, white nongovernmental-organization-affiliated ones—who she thought, because they appeared to have never missed a meal in their lives, were rich. It didn't matter to her that most of the time she had no idea what they were saying. Trying to make sense of their native languages was a delightful game to her. By repeating some of the things they said, she thought she was learning English, Spanish, Portuguese, French, German, or whatever language they spoke. Still, in trying to keep the guests happy, the night concierge did not discourage her. The time she spent with these men never seemed to him to last long enough for her to have had sex with them anyway. Besides, she was living with her mother, who was always watching her.

Mélisande stopped crying because she seemed to have run out of tears. And now she had the hiccups, which forced her head to jerk back and forth toward and away from me.

"We have to find you a place where you can get a second opinion," I told her.

She raised her head and glared at me, then she opened her eyes wide, as though a beehive or a bird's nest had suddenly appeared on top of my head. Her eyes were bright red, the bulging capillaries having taken over her eyeballs.

"They told me there was no cure," she said.

"Let me talk to Mesye Xavier," I said. "We'll find you some care."

I had no idea where to find the best treatment in Port-au-Prince, but I knew Xavier would. He knew something about nearly everything, especially things that involved worst-case-scenario types of problems. This is in part a guide and hotelier's job. If guests show up hungry, you feed them. If they want drink, you ply them. If they want to be left alone, you make yourself scarce. If they want company, you entertain. If they are lovelorn, you find them love. And if they show up sick, you find them treatment quickly before they expire on your watch.

Wesley tested negative for HIV. The same Canadian doctor who performed his tests and

Mélisande's second test in Pétionville was the one who'd help us get the retroviral drugs that Mélisande needed. The best thing, he told us, was a one-pill treatment many of his patients were calling the gwo blan, or the big white. It made compliance easier. Mélisande, he could already tell, was not going to be compliant. First of all, she was claiming she'd never had sex with anyone, and since she had not injected herself with hypodermic needles and had not had blood transfusions, all he could conclude was that she was in terrible denial.

"If you won't even own up to the possible ways the disease might have entered your body, how can you hope to treat this disease aggressively?" he'd told Mélisande in French-accented Creole as she sat across a desk from him, her eyelids fluttering between open and closed, staring, when they were open, at a wall full of diplomas.

But once the doctor provided us with two months' worth of pills from his own private stash—at two American dollars a pill— Mélisande was more compliant than any of us expected. To get her started, I told her to come and find me every morning so I could watch her take the pill as we ate breakfast together, usually something solid like plantains and eggs or spaghetti with herring for her, and something light, coffee and toast, for me. Most of the time we ate on the patio of my room, which overlooked the hotel pool, where a few of our guests would already be having their morning swim. Other times we ate in the hotel dining room with Wesley in a high chair at my side.

Mélisande began to gain weight, my old clothes fitting her better now. She cried less, too, in part, I think, because she knew the whole staff, including the groundsman and security guard, were watching us. But what she never did again was touch my son, who reached his tubby little arms out to her, contorting his face into a grimace that would turn into wails, then tears, when she simply ignored him or turned away.

I stopped bringing Wesley to breakfast with her after a while. It was too much for both of them. Though I surely needed one, I didn't hire another nanny because I didn't want Mélisande feeling worse than she already did. Instead I asked Xavier to pitch in a little more when he didn't have any tours and took Wesley with me everywhere, pushing him around in a stroller when he became too heavy to carry.

That particular week, my problem guests included the young local newly married couple who'd spent four nights locked up in our honeymoon suite when they had only reserved it for two. And the senator who'd abandoned his house for security reasons and was now living in one of the rooms next to the gazebo.

I came across the senator as I sprinted around with Wesley, hastily inspecting the grounds before having breakfast with Mélisande. The senator was sitting by the pool reading his newspaper while wearing only his swimming trunks. He smiled and winked like he always did whenever I reminded him of his unpaid bill. There was also the hunchbacked elderly French philosopher. He claimed to be writing a book about Haiti, but I had never seen him do anything but smoke and drink heavily at all hours of the day. Along with the stringer who had to be reminded that the money her newspaper had supposedly wired had never arrived, each of these guests required some nudging. Much more nudging than Mélisande, who I felt confident would now be fine taking her medication on her own.

I soon stopped the breakfasts altogether and passed on the job of monitoring Mélisande's compliance to her mother, who from the day she learned Mélisande was sick started calling her a bouzen, a whore, even as she stopped whatever she was doing every morning to make sure that her daughter swallowed the pill with breakfast.

Some mornings I'd watch them from the patio. Babette was no taller than Mélisande, but was strapping and thick. The veins in her short neck throbbed as she continuously berated Mélisande, who'd try to put an end to their interaction by swallowing the pill, then dashing off.

"What will you do when mesye and madame stop paying for your hundred-gourde pills?" Babette would shout like a drill sergeant hazing a recruit. Her fear was palpable. Her daughter's survival now depended on my husband and me. If we decided to sell the hotel and move elsewhere, her child could get sicker. What if the drug companies stopped making the drug or no longer sent it to Haiti? If any part of the chain that ran from the creation of the drug to our ability to afford it broke down, she might lose her child.

One morning, I heard Babette asking Mélisande as she was taking the pill, "What if the foreigners, the blan, start keeping the medikaman for themselves? What if mesye and madame leave Haiti?"

"You will never have a healthy child," she told her another day. "You will never have a husband."

"You should talk to her," Xavier said to me after overhearing this.

He was preparing a dinner for a group of local businessmen who sometimes used the hotel conference room for their meetings. He was making notes on his phone about ordering wines, alerting the chef, and coming up with a menu as he spoke.

"It can't be helpful for the poor girl to be treated that way," he said.

"Where do you want to be buried?" Babette said soon after. "You better start saving if you want a fancy coffin."

Unlike the rest of us, Babette couldn't afford the conditional optimism this pill allowed. If Mélisande were my daughter and I could barely afford these pills, I might have had the same fears.

The next morning, I asked to have a word with Babette, who, as soon as I closed my husband's office door behind us, grabbed my hand and said, "Mèsi, mèsi. Thank you, madame, for not throwing her out. Thank you for not letting her die."

"There are people all over the world taking this medication," I said, gently tugging my hand out of her grasp. "Besides, you're wasting precious time with your daughter, time you could be spending with her just as you had before. You can help her the most by not cursing but loving her."

"Love her?" She frowned, moving a few steps away from me.

"Yes, love her," I said. It must have sounded like an order. "You must love her," I stressed.

I knew what she was thinking. These half-assed outsiders, these no-longer-fully-Haitian, almost-blan, foreigner-type people, these dyaspora with their mushy thinking, why does it all come back to one kind of love with them, the kind of love you keep talking about rather than the kind of love that shatters you to pieces? Don't these die-ass-poor-aahs, these dyaspowa and dyasporèn, these outside-minded kings and queens, know that there are many other ways to show love than to be constantly talking about it?

"Of course I love her," she said, spreading

both her arms wide open as if to illustrate how much. "That's why I am so rough with her."

She lowered her gaze and bowed her head and appeared ashamed that I, on top of everything, had reason to scold her, ashamed that she had no choice but to stand there and take it.

"Eskize m. I'm sorry," I said. "We're both mothers. I understand."

She looked around the room, at the framed photographs on the wall, at the pictures of Xavier's and my family members, both in Haiti and far away. She looked at the close-to-a-dozen pictures of Wesley's less than a year on this earth. She looked at the wall as though she was hoping to see herself or Mélisande there, but was still not surprised that she didn't.

"You're a mother who can provide not only for your own child, but mine, too," she said, turning her eyes toward the white ceiling. "We're not the same."

I wanted Mélisande to be healthy, I told her, and so did she. In that way, we were the same. I knew she was not convinced. I also knew that even after our talk there would be no apologies or reconciliatory mother-and-daughter embrace between her and Mélisande.

The next morning, I watched from the patio

where Wesley was bobbing up and down in a playpen next to me and saw her silently hand Mélisande a glass of water.

"Whatever did you tell her?" Xavier asked as he looked in on Wesley.

"You know . . . ," I said, which he realized meant that I didn't want to talk about it.

At the end of the second month, when Mélisande needed a refill of the drugs, her doctor left Haiti and moved back to Montreal. Mélisande had no choice but to start seeing another doctor, a Cuban one this time, who ordered a new series of tests. When Mélisande came back with several bottles of pills, including herbal pills and vitamins, I could tell that whatever illusion she'd harbored about having gotten better was gone.

The new regimen did not agree with her. She had stomachaches, nausea, and diarrhea and spent her days in bed. It would take time for her body to get used to the drug and supplements, the Cuban doctor said, but she needed them both, not just the retroviral but also the natural stuff. Xavier made a few more calls, and we found Mélisande yet another doctor, a Haitian female one, to confirm that Mélisande was indeed getting the right treatment.

After the doctor examined her in the room she and her mother shared, Mélisande told the doctor that she wanted the one-pill treatment back. She handed the prescription bottles from the Canadian doctor to the Haitian female doctor, who sucked her teeth loudly and exclaimed "Jesus, Marie, Joseph!" when she saw the Canadian doctor's name.

"What's wrong?" I asked from where I was standing by the door.

It turned out, the Haitian woman doctor elaborated, that what Mélisande had gotten from the Canadian doctor was less potent than an aspirin. It was a placebo. It had not been doing anything for her at all. In fact, it might have even weakened her immune system. The Canadian doctor who had prescribed and sold the first pills to us had fled Haiti because he'd been discovered by some colleagues who'd reported him to the Ministry of Health for selling those useless pills to dozens of unsuspecting patients all over the city. There was even some doubt as to whether he was a doctor at all.

"You must be extra vigilant," the doctor told Mélisande. She prescribed the gwo blan again, but told us to make sure we got the real thing. Mélisande's body sank deeper under her bedsheets when she heard the news. She had lost precious time.

"He was playing with her life," the doctor told me as I walked out of the room with her. Mélisande turned her face away from us, burying it in her pillow while I pulled the door shut behind us.

I shouldn't have been so trustful of the first doctor. Maybe I was blinded by the white skin and all the diplomas on his wall. Would I have been so willing to trust him if Mélisande had been my daughter?

"We've gone way beyond the call of duty," Xavier said while texting a driver about a visit to MUPANAH, the national museum, with a group of Haitian American art students in a few days.

"How?" I asked. "By getting her a quack?"

"We tried," he said.

"We failed," I shouted.

"We did everything we would have done for Wesley," he said.

"Did we?"

I immediately made an appointment for our son to have a second test.

· · ·

That afternoon before Wesley's doctor's appointment, Mélisande's mother served Xavier and me lunch in the gazebo while our son napped in his stroller. She was sweating in her light blue uniform. Her head was wrapped in a black scarf, and though this was what she wore most days, it suddenly looked like mourning garb.

"We're sorry," Xavier told her. "But she was probably sick before she came to us. It could have happened when she was even younger."

She lay the food down quickly, turned her back to us without saying anything, and walked away. Perhaps she considered us just as deceitful as the quack, and now we were insulting her child, too.

I should apologize to her, I told Xavier after she left, reassure her that we were trying to help Mélisande. We had been duped, not just out of our money but out of hope.

I got up to go find Mélisande's mother, but Xavier grabbed my hand and pulled me down.

"Leave it alone," he said, now sounding truly angry, not only at the deceitful and perhaps fake doctor, and at the entire situation, but at Mélisande's mother, too.

.   .   .

A few days later, I went to their room to see Mélisande to tell her that Wesley's second test had also come back negative. She was lying in bed in a deep sleep and did not stir when I walked in the room. Her newly plaited waist-length box braids seemed too bulky for her face and were fanned out around her head like a nest of fleeing snakes. Her still-fragile-looking body, now stripped bare except for a black bra and polka-dotted panties, would eventually adjust completely, the doctor had told us.

Watching her sleep so quietly, and so exposed, especially with her mouth open, I thought what will she possessed. Her symptoms had completely disappeared for nearly two months while she was taking that ineffectual pill. It seemed to help once she'd believed it could. There was something different about her face now, though. She no longer looked young. Perhaps it was because of her erratic weight loss and gain, but she even had wrinkles, some between her eyebrows, some around her mouth.

A week later, Mélisande got out of bed again. I noticed her one morning sitting fully dressed in a lounge chair by the pool and staring into the water while Wesley and I were having breakfast on the patio. She reached into her skirt pocket and pulled out a small piece of jewelry that she traced against the lifelines in her palm. She then made a fist around it before placing it in her pocket again. She did this a couple of times, pulled the thing out of her pocket, then looked down at it, then put it back. At some point I noticed it was a ring, with a shiny gem that, though minute, was still drawing more light to it than the rest.

I walked Wesley down to the pool to see her. Her eyes were closed, and I had to call out her name to let her know we were there. She was surprised to see us.

"How are you?" I asked while we slid into the lounge chair next to hers.

My son lunged for the shiny trinket, which was in Mélisande's left hand, but she pulled both hands away and shoved it back into her pocket.

"What's that?" I asked.

Mélisande must have been wondering how long I had been looking at her, watching her pull this thing in and out of her pocket. Slowly she reached in deeper and out came the ring once more. The gold was as thin as spaghetti but it had, just as I'd suspected, a small glass stone that was capturing the light. Drawn by the glint of the stone, Wesley reached for the ring once more, but Mélisande yanked it away again as if to protect it from his grasp.

"Did one of the guests leave that behind?" I asked her.

She shook her head no.

"Did someone give it to you?"

She nodded.

"A man?"

Another nod.

"Did he give it to you before you were sick?"

"Maybe," she answered softly while keeping her eyes on the fist now closed tightly around the ring.

"He said he was going to marry you?"

She said nothing.

He did say he would marry her, I suspected, then he left and returned home to his life, or his wife, or whoever it was he was truly beholden to, and he never came back.

The ring was worthless, of course, one of the fake-gold krizokal ones made by the corner jeweler down the street. I had seen a bunch of them on the fingers of young girls who came to the hotel for drinks and sexual exploits with both foreign and local guests, guests who told them

they loved them and gave them a ring like this
as a symbol of their loyalty, then left them clinging to some hollow promise and never looked
back. Around the hotel, those types of rings
even had a name. We called them the Port-au-
Prince marriage special, renmen m, kite m—or
love-me-and-leave-me—rings.

"Mélisande," I began, trying to think of the
best way to tell her, or to remind her, that this
ring was like the pills she'd been taking at first.
There was no truth, magic, or healing in it. Her
sunken face and reddened eyes indicated that
she already knew.

"M konnen," she said, "I know," signaling
with a wave of her bony hands that she no longer wanted to talk about it.

The Gift

Anika promised Thomas a gift so he would have dinner with her on the Fourth of July. They hadn't seen each other in over seven months, not since before the earthquake. The glass-walled restaurant overlooking Biscayne Bay was her idea. They had eaten there many times before and, in much-happier days, had both found the dim lighting and black leather couches not just intriguing but also romantic. The crate-style coffee tables on which the meals were served had always been a challenge, but the breathtaking view of the downtown Miami skyline kept them coming back. It was a good place to watch the Fourth of July fireworks, and in spite of how crowded the restaurant would eventually get, the corner where they always sat would be quiet enough for them to talk.

Anika had bought a special dress for the

occasion, a black halter mini that grazed her thighs. When Thomas arrived, he looked nothing like the dapper man she once loved, the one she'd been attracted to from the moment they'd met, when she appeared at his real estate office, a penthouse suite overlooking downtown Miami, and asked if she could decorate the walls of his offices with her clients' paintings, on the condition that he help her sell the paintings to his renters or buyers or their interior decorators.

"Don't know about all that," he'd said, smirking, even as his blonde female assistant was sitting next to her, across the desk from him, taking notes. "Besides, it would be a lot of work. You'd have to be here all the time, looking after those paintings. And after me."

He was still new to Miami then, a double dyaspora from both Park Slope, USA, and Pacot, Haiti. Back then, he was spending a lot of time at the gym. As he approached the table, he looked less burly and much thinner, and an inch or so shorter.

He slid down onto the couch and wrapped his arms around her neck. He smelled like one of the many aftershaves he took turns using, in spite of her recommendation that he stick to just one so that whenever she smelled it, wherever she happened to be, she would think of him.

"People don't remember smells," she'd told him, "unless the smells are tied to something or someone—"

She'd meant to say: something or someone they love. But she knew this wasn't always true. People also associate some smells with things they hate or are trying to forget.

After saying hello, he kept his arms around her neck for so long that she had no choice but to stroke his back. She patted it midspine just as she would if he were crying. In times past, he would have been wearing some designer jeans and a dark T-shirt, but now it was a long-sleeved white shirt and plain dark slacks. On his right ear was a tiny diamond earring, which looked as though it might belong to a baby girl.

"That's new," she said, pointing at the earring.

"As is so much else." He pulled away from her and pressed his back into the sofa. He sat up straight, almost too straight, like he'd been caught doing something wrong.

She was the one who'd pursued him. He agreed over time to buy her clients' paintings as housewarming gifts for his. Each time he bought a

painting from her, she treated him to a celebratory dinner in this same restaurant. His
confidence, his cockiness, were what had won
her over. She'd found his flirting with her in
another woman's presence, even the ones who
worked for him in his office, sexy. He was captivating, extremely photogenic, with his bald
head and mahogany-colored skin. His voice was
radio deep, as though every time he opened his
mouth he was making on-air announcements.

"I'm surprised you called me back this time,"
she said.

"It's a holiday and I had nothing to do,"
he said.

"There've been other holidays."

"Ones that mattered?"

"This one matters to you?"

"We're here, aren't we?"

"You came because I promised you something."

"We've always promised each other things,"
he said. "Well, not always **things.**"

He looked around the room, which was becoming more and more crowded. Voices grew
from whispers to normal talk, then the occasional shout of someone trying to be heard.
Many of the other patrons were already angling
for empty spots next to the glass walls, which

were high above the bottlenecked Brickell Avenue Bridge. It had taken some convincing, and reminding the manager how much money they'd spent there, to get their usual table.

"I do like the Fourth of July," he said. "I barely remember what we did last year, though."

"I got the midday picnic in my apartment. She got the fireworks at Bayfront Park."

"Which was a mistake," he said. "The fireworks terrified my daughter."

He never said their names to her, neither the wife's nor the daughter's. It was as though he wanted them to remain fuzzy, abstract, vague.

She learned a few weeks after they met that he had a wife and baby. After he sold a multimillion-dollar mansion to a new star player for the Miami Heat, he was profiled in the business section of the **Miami Times.** He had moved to New York with his family at age nine. His wife was born into a well-to-do Haitian clan and had relocated to Miami as an adult. Her family was in the construction trade in Haiti, and he wanted to enter the market there. It was a perfect fit.

The picture of the three of them on the newspaper's website—him, his wife, his infant daughter—sitting in their luxurious Miami penthouse's living room, hit her like an assault. There they were. Holy trinity. Perfect family. The wife's mix of Lebanese and Haitian ancestry showed in her russet-colored skin and cascade of thick Cleopatra-style hair. Their daughter, nearly a year old, was doughy, edible looking, her pudgy arms wrapped around the wife's jeweled neck.

Thomas now slid his body close to hers until there was nowhere else for him to go. When he rested his head on her shoulder, she reached into her bag for her cell phone. She was going to call a girlfriend to come rescue her so she wouldn't be tempted to backtrack or change her mind or slip into old ways after dinner. Watching her drop her cell phone back in her purse, he said, "I was at the Caribbean Market in Port-au-Prince once, and all of the maids were on their cell phones with their mistresses. I should put that differently, with their bosses. And then the maids got on the phone with **their** maids to tell them what to cook their kids for lunch."

When she narrowed her eyes and looked perplexed, he added, "After the earthquake, didn't you hear about all the people who were stuck under houses and schools, and the Caribbean

Market, texting for help on their cell phones, for hours?"

"Did you have your phone with you when the house fell?" she asked.

He raised his head from her shoulder, and Anika felt the much-lighter weight of him slip away.

"For once, no," he said. "I was trying to focus on family. But I wish I did have my phone with me down there."

"You look good," she said when he failed to elaborate. She was lying. His gaunt face was full of nicks and scars that, if he were clever with makeup, he might be able to cover.

The busboy came by with water, then the waiter with silverware and a menu, but these people might as well have been shadows, ghosts. There was a speech about specials and the menu that she was too distracted to hear well. She had memorized the menu anyway.

"We need a minute," he said when asked what he was drinking.

"We might as well eat on the floor," he said the same way he had in the past, while tapping the crate coffee table with his palms.

When the waiter came back, Thomas ordered the same Chilean Pinot Noir they'd always had, the one with the peppery taste and earthy aroma. It was their favorite. He also ordered some prawns and crab cakes.

"Have you been working?" he asked, once the waiter was gone. "Are you still selling a lot of pieces?"

"I lost my best client, remember?" she said.

"That's right. Me," he said, while patting himself on the shoulders.

"I'm working with a few interior decorators," she said. "Kind of a step down, but I'm also doing some sketching now myself, some simple line drawings."

She knew he was doing his best to catch up. She wanted to tell him that she was still living in the nearby condo where he used to visit her, that the bedroom was still small, and that the terrace, packed with her collection of colorful patio chairs, still overlooked both the MacArthur Causeway and Biscayne Bay. She wanted to tell him that she was still teaching that Intro to Art History class at Miami Dade College twice a week, and that what she was sketching now, from photographs, in notebook-sized drawing pads, was a series of birds. Her favorites were the Antillean mango birds, the only birds known to fly backward. She was also sketching a lot of striped-bellied piculets, the kind whose feathers had been found buried in twenty-five-million-year-old amber in the Dominican Republic.

The waiter came back with the wine, and Thomas made a show of sniffing and tasting it. Clicking his full glass against hers, he said, "Santé."

"To better days." She took a gulp, then put her glass down.

The appetizers came and kept coming and they both looked down at them, uninterested. She wondered what it might be like to be in bed now with this new version of him, the one who was missing a left leg from the knee down, though she could hardly tell which one of his legs was the prosthesis. She wanted to believe that it would be easy to take things up right where they had left off, that the yearning she'd once had for his strong if pampered body, the hunger, would still be there. But she wasn't sure. She could tell that some of his confidence was gone. Yet perhaps the loss of confidence had less to do with the leg and more with everything and everyone he'd lost. She wanted to see, to experience, the absent part of his body, this leg, just as she had when it was still walking toward and away from her bed, or when it was still wrapped tightly around her body. She thought that he might bend down at any time, pull up his pant leg, and show her his prosthesis. Instead he grabbed a crab cake from a small plate and began shoving it in his mouth. He took his time chewing while she watched his face, his now messier and older-looking face.

"Have you been to Haiti since . . . ," she asked.

He didn't answer at first and seemed to be trying to stuff his words down his throat as he grabbed another crab cake, which he washed down with the whole glass of wine.

"Non" was finally all he said when his mouth, too, was empty.

The afternoon of the earthquake, she had been at Miami Dade College teaching. She'd grown close to some of her students that semester, and they'd invited her to a dinner the Haitian students' association was hosting. They had also invited a popular local Haitian singer named Roro as the entertainment.

After she left the class, she was considering not attending the dinner. Then her phone started ringing. And with everyone she loved being far away, with her parents living in Brooklyn, and with other relatives in Paris, Santo Domingo, and Montreal worried but accounted for, and with Thomas on a prolonged New Year's holiday with his wife and daughter in Haiti and not answering his phone, she decided to go to the student dinner after all. What better time to be with other people? she'd thought. There were still no detailed reports.

The college reception hall was packed. When she walked in, hundreds of students and faculty were sitting in a wide circle on what was supposed to be the dance floor. The singer Roro, the closest thing to a spiritual leader in sight, was standing in the middle of the circle. Towering over everyone, he seemed lost nonetheless, flabbergasted, his hands clasped together, his face crumpled. The student association president, an anxious young woman, walked over to Roro. Sobbing, she asked him to continue his ritual.

If only rituals could instantly heal us, Anika had thought. While waiting to see what Roro would come up with, she repeatedly checked Thomas's and his wife's social media pages and linked to the pages of their friends and their friends' friends. There were no updates, just a stream of expressions of concern and worry.

When his Miami real estate office was

reopened by his colleagues a week later, his assistant told her about his wife and daughter dying and his left leg being amputated at the knee joint. He was back in the States, but no one was supposed to know where. His cell phone was disconnected. He had returned to the office just a few days ago, when he finally took her call.

When the waiter came around again, Thomas ordered more food that he kept eating, small things he was picking up with his hands, empanadas, buffalo wings. She was too nervous to eat, but he didn't seem to notice.

"I'm craving akra," he said, perhaps recalling the fried malaga fritters she used to cook for him.

"I could make that," she expected herself to say, but she didn't. Just as she didn't want to give in to her hankering to invite him over to her place. And who said he'd want to go anyway? It had taken him months to answer her phone calls.

"I've been missing this kind of food," he said.

"You were so careful about your diet before," she said.

"I was careful with some things and careless

with others," he said. "Besides, you're the one who wanted to come here. We occasionally ate things like this here. Not just the salads."

"Not all at the same time," she said.

"You're not eating." He finally noticed. "Drink more. You'll be happier."

"I'm not exactly thinking about being happy right now," she said.

"You should be," he said. "Isn't that what these fireworks are about? The American right to happiness and all of that."

She started sketching million-year-old birds because she couldn't imagine how to sketch or paint what she really wanted to, earthquakes. Her sketches were meant to be studies for paintings, but she got no further than that. When you paint an earthquake, do you paint soil monsters devouring the earth? Shattered houses? Bloody, lifeless bodies? Random personal items—T-shirts, dresses, shoes, hair combs, and toothbrushes—scattered above the rubble? Do you paint cemeteries and grave markers and distraught mourners weeping over them? Do you paint crosses, wilted dust-covered flowers, or vibrant bright red ones, for hope? Do you write messages on your canvases, in case anyone misses the point? Or do you sketch your lover, his dead wife, and their dead baby daughter? A derivative, photo-realistic work based on an online image, something so faithful to the original that it could easily be mistaken for it, except in your sketches their high-end designer clothes become feathers, and apart from their legs and faces, they become birds.

Now she could also paint a man stuffing his face while regretting having come to a dinner he had long put off.

"Where were you all this time?" she finally asked him, in case he—or she—got up at any point in the evening and fled. "You said you'd tell me tonight."

During their first phone call a few days before, he'd told her that she could ask him everything she wanted to at dinner. Pushing the food aside, he chuckled nervously, then said, "Physical rehab, where I still go. Also a nuthouse. I spent time in a nuthouse."

"A psychiatric hospital?"

"We have a winner." He raised his hands up in the air and cheered sarcastically.

"I'm sorry," she said, "I didn't know."

She reached for his back. He pulled away.

"You weren't meant to know," he said. "No one was meant to know."

When his assistant told her he was doing therapy somewhere and didn't want to talk to anyone, she thought only about the amputated leg, the prosthesis. She hadn't considered his mind, that he'd be so broken that he would also need this other kind of help.

"Some guys I'd come to know in Port-au-Prince," he said as he reached for more food. "Their bodies were found crushed together with their mistresses in hotel rooms. How would it have looked if my wife and child were pulled out in pieces from under her parents' house, I'm taken out from under the house alive, and I continue this thing with you?"

That's the bargain he'd made over the hours of waiting, with whichever gods had heard their breaths grow more and more shallow alongside him, he said. And when nighttime came and when the aftershocks continued and when both his wife and daughter fell silent in the dark, he swore that, if they were spared and he didn't die, he would never speak to Anika again.

She picked up her wineglass and tried to picture some ghostly and shadowy version of this, of his leg crushed beneath one of the house beams, of his wife and daughter at first screaming for help, then losing blood, strength, hope, then breath. Then she saw the people who had been digging for the three of them finding only him alive. Barely alive, as his assistant had said.

"So how would it look if after all that I kept sleeping with you?" he repeated.

"How would it **look**?" she said, before stopping herself from saying more. Did he think that theirs was ever a moral love? Otherwise, how could she explain the initial twinge of delight she'd felt when she'd learned that his wife and daughter had died? Was it actually glee she'd felt? Or was it yet another version of the fantasy she'd nurtured for nearly a year, of his wife and child disappearing, allowing her to take their place?

"I wasn't ever going to leave them for you," he said, as if responding to her thoughts. He turned his face toward the causeway and the glass towers and skyscrapers, whose reflections created, as the night sky darkened, a parallel city on the water. "And you were not the only one," he added, his voice growing colder as he went along. "I think you should know that there were other women."

She tried to speak, but her own voice cracked, and the sound fell back into her throat. Aside from the need to let him go, what she was feeling most was shame. He was direct, even brutal sometimes, yet he could be gentle, too, she reminded herself. She remembered him rushing around her apartment and hurriedly jumping into his clothes when he really wanted to stay.

"Five more minutes," he'd say while slipping under the covers in her bed, five minutes that would sometimes turn into five more hours, which as time went by would require bigger and bigger lies to explain his absence to his wife. During these moments, she'd felt that nothing real could grow out of their betrayal, which had been complicated by her wanting to have a baby. He must have wanted that, too, she told herself, because in spite of making a halfhearted effort at precautions, she got pregnant anyway.

"Is there anything else you'd like to know?" he asked.

Was there anything else **he** wanted to know? she wondered.

He was fidgeting, rubbing his hands together. He seemed nervous, angry even. His sudden mood change scared her. Maybe his head wasn't fully right yet. Or he wasn't ready to tell her all those things. Perhaps that's why he had stayed away.

"Please don't ask me if I loved her," he said. "Because you won't like my answer."

"Of course you loved her," she said.

"Then what was I doing with you?"

"I guess you loved me, too. How could anyone not love me?" she said, trying to tease him even now, while laughing a bit at herself.

But plenty of other men had not loved her, and she had not loved them, either. It was too much time, too much work. Their desire for permanence drove her away. Once they wanted to live with her, to move in, to marry, she would lose interest. Except this time, this man, him. She remained interested.

The night of the earthquake, at the college hall, the singer Roro asked if anyone happened to have a rope. No one did, so some men offered their neckties and a few women their scarves. Roro asked for help in tying the ties and few scarves together until they formed a table-sized cloth circle in the middle of the room.

"This is now the epicenter of the earthquake," Roro said. "And we are going to fill it with our love."

This was not exactly what she'd wanted, needed. And nearly everyone seemed as disappointed as she was that Roro had not provided them with a more meaningful ritual, with unique and specific prayers, hymns or psalms to recite, or soothing refrains to chant. This was supposed to be their spontaneous porta fidei, their transient door of faith, their sudden sanctuary. This thing with the epicenter ties and scarves felt trite to her, empty, untrue. But it was their incantation of the moment, until some more ancient ceremonies could be recalled in detail or newer ones devised. Another type of priest, cantor, vicar, or layperson might have performed a different ritual, but the basic idea would have been the same: to try, with will and desire alone, to influence something you could not.

One of the students went out and came back with a bottle of Haitian rum, and while pouring it in the middle of the circle, Roro made everyone recite over and over "Pou sa n pa wè yo."

Anika, too, had joined in, mouthing, though not really wanting to, "Pou sa n pa wè yo. For those we don't see. For those who are not here."

. . .

The restaurant was filling up, and the waiter's visits to their table became less frequent. They were now both drinking more than they were eating. The bottle of wine was empty.

The way his assistant had told it, his in-laws' neighbors had a stocked liquor cabinet that had somehow survived the earthquake. They'd brought everything they had to the field hospital, where his leg was amputated at the knee joint. He had gulped down a bottle of thirty-year-old scotch before a surgeon friend cut off his crushed left leg. There had been no hope for the leg and not enough time to airlift him, or get him to a hospital out of the country for a more sterile procedure.

"When you called, you said you had a gift for me." He was looking at her again, and his eyes began to seem more familiar, full of playfulness and desire. He was acting as though what he'd said, about never having intended to leave his wife while also being with other women, didn't matter. He held his hands out to her, as though waiting for her to produce the gift. She let his hands dangle until he pulled them away and stuck them in his pockets.

In the past when she was in this restaurant with him, she used to wish that she had met him before he'd met his wife. But then she would have been the wife, and he would have cheated on her, and not just with one person, as he'd just told her, but with many other women. She didn't believe there had been other women besides her and his wife, though. If that were true, he wouldn't have blurted it out like that.

"Why'd you really want to see me?" he asked now.

She wanted to fashion some answer that would sound reasonable. "I wanted to give you a gift. I also wanted to tell you about our baby that never was, our spirit child. I thought seeing you would make me realize that no one is worth wishing two people dead for."

The gift was in her apartment. She had imagined some scenario where she would have him wait in his car, and she'd bring it down to him before they said their final goodbye. She did not want to see him react to it. She didn't want him to talk to her about it. She didn't want to know whether he'd keep it or throw it away.

"I wanted to see you because I thought we should end this face-to-face," she said.

"It ended when they died," he said. "You must know that. We didn't have to see each other for that."

He tilted his head back as though offering her his throat to cut, then he spread his hand over the front of his neck to protect it. Seeing her, she knew, was shattering him again. She was one of many offenses he would struggle to forgive himself for. She'd even felt this a few months back when she kept calling him, to both offer her condolences and tell him about their baby, and he would not answer her calls.

It wasn't that devastating as far as miscarriages go. She was tired after a class and drifted off to sleep that evening, just as the sun was setting over the bay. A few hours later, she woke up with her pelvis cramping so much that it felt as though it was hammering itself into her back. She started spotting, and then there were some clots, then it was full-on bleeding. She drove herself to a nearby emergency room at midnight, and a few hours later was told that she'd had an "inevitable" miscarriage.

"Why inevitable?" she asked the young, exhausted-looking obstetrics intern on call.

"That's the medical term," he said. "Your cervix was dilated and your fetus had no heartbeat. There was no other possible outcome."

.   .   .

The Fourth of July fireworks were about to begin now. Some of the patrons were making their way to the glass wall. Others went up to the roof lounge. She held out her hand to him to help him to his feet. He was up faster than she expected. He pushed aside the crate table, moving ahead of her. When he reached the wall, he formed a triangle with his back, the concrete wall, and the glass. He then stepped aside and allowed her to slip between his arms, even as more and more people were crowding in.

The fireworks began with a single exploding red star, which burst into a trail of red, white, and blue streaks. His knees buckled against hers. His body tensed up. He wrapped his arms around her waist, not to embrace her but to hold himself up. He was shaking. His quivering lips brushed against her ear. He was saying something she couldn't quite make out. Then he pressed down on her shoulder with both his hands and turned her body around.

"The ground is moving," he shouted in her ear.

His face was sweating, his breath racing. The building, it now felt to her, too, was vibrating as the fireworks grew louder and more elaborate. She worried that the glass wouldn't hold and that she, he, and all the other people there would fall several stories into the bay.

"I need to get out of here," he mouthed. He might have been yelling, but the words were trapped in his mouth.

"Let's go back," she said.

She held both his hands as they moved away. The people closest to them noticed that something was wrong and stepped aside to make room for them to pass. He kept his hands in hers as she guided him toward their table.

She motioned for one of the waiters to bring her some water quickly, and he returned with a glass bottle. Thomas tried to slow down his breathing by inhaling deeply through his nose, then pushing the air out of his mouth. It was obviously not the first time this had happened to him.

As she poured him a glass from the water bottle, he caught his breath long enough to say, "If this was a Haitian restaurant, I'd pour some water on my head."

"Why would it have to be a Haitian restaurant?" she asked.

"My people would understand."

"Who says you can't do that here?" she asked.

Looking down at the bottle and at the full glass in front of him, she said, "I dare you."

"Do you really?"

He picked up the glass, then slowly poured the water over his bald head. As the water slid down his face, he tried to catch some with his tongue before it crawled down his chin onto the front of his shirt.

"Your turn," he told her, making no attempts to wipe the water.

"Are you insane?" she asked.

"Apparently." He dangled the bottle over her head, waiting for some word from her to either pour it or not. The fireworks show was over, and some of the patrons were returning to their tables.

"If you're going to do it, do it," she said.

The water felt ice cold against her hair, flattening it. It dripped down past her bare shoulder, through her bra, and down her stomach.

"Okay, you can stop now," she said, wiping her face with her hands. By the time he lowered the bottle, it was empty.

She hated herself for how happy she felt sitting there, soaking wet in her brand-new dress. They were now a spectacle that some of the

other patrons were watching, some with envy
at their apparent joie de vivre and others clearly
disapproving. She told herself he needed her
in a way he hadn't before, to protect him from
loud noises and shaking buildings, to keep him
out of the nuthouse, as he called it. But even
that was a weak excuse. She was there now, just
as she'd been before, because she wanted to be.
And maybe neither one of them was worthy
of moments like this, but she wanted more
of them.

Their waiter walked over and handed them a
few extra cloth napkins.

"I'm sorry I lost it over there." His face grew
somber again, though not as much as when he'd
been fleeing the fireworks. "I felt like Qadine
out at Bayfront Park last year."

Qadine was the name of his daughter. Dina
was his wife. It was the first time he'd ever mentioned his daughter to her by name.

"My head was exploding just now," he said.

"I had no idea what I was going to do with
you," she said.

The waiter returned with their check. Thomas
insisted on paying and added a large tip.

"So what will you do with me now?" he asked.

. . .

Water was still dripping off of them as they walked the three blocks to her apartment. The streets were packed with postfireworks crowds, which, along with his slower gait, made the walk back to her place take twice as long as usual.

Walking into her apartment, he seemed relaxed, even while looking over the crowded living room, her packed bookshelves, her old gray sofa and chaise longue, and her pair of rustic floor lamps.

"Would you like something to drink?" she asked.

"Not water," he said.

Somewhere in her kitchen was a bottle of Chilean Pinot Noir from the last time they'd seen each other. He had enjoyed the wine so much that he convinced their waitress to sell him an unopened bottle. He'd left the wine in her apartment to drink during a future visit, which never took place.

She was thinking of bringing the bottle out when he said, "Never mind. I think I'm done with liquids for tonight." Then he began undressing. He unbuttoned, then peeled off, his wet shirt, then his white undershirt, which he dropped on the floor. He unbuckled his belt and let his pants fall to his ankles.

"I can throw them in the dryer," she said as she bent down to pick up the clothes.

"No need." He sounded so certain that she put them down again.

Now in only his plaid boxer shorts, with his pants at his feet, he lowered himself and sat on her carpeted floor. His body was scarred all over, she noticed, with tears, dips, folds, keloids, and patches on his back, stomach, and thighs, where he'd been bruised, scratched, pricked, or had lost layers of skin. Sitting on the floor, he raised first his own leg out of the pants, then the prosthetic.

The prosthetic looked nearly identical to his other leg, the dark surface skinlike. He twisted what looked to her like a silicone mold, looping it back and forth, then pulled it off at the knee. It came off with a puff, a reverse-suction sound. Underneath was a bulging ball of dark skin, with a track of scarring that looked like it had been made with staples.

"You wanted to see," he said. "I could tell."

She hadn't expected to **see** that way. She slid down and sat next to him, the amputated leg lying limply on the carpet between them. She heard his breath racing again; this time, it seemed, from embarrassment or self-pity.

"Can I touch it?" she asked.

He said nothing, so she reached over and tapped her fingers gently against the rounded tip, then ran her palm over the jagged skin, where his knee bone rested. In some spots, the nub felt slippery like glass, in others doughy, like warm bread. She was afraid to touch the suture marks, which, because of the gaps of lighter skin peeking out between them, made the rest of the leg still look unhealed.

"Seen enough?" he asked.

He didn't wait for her to answer. He brushed her hand away and reached for the prosthetic, pushed, it seemed to her, the absent leg into it, and quickly popped it back in place. He then put on his wet clothes, more slowly than he had taken them off. First the pants, then the undershirt, then the shirt.

When he was fully dressed, he held the wall and stood up. She stood up, too.

How could she have thought that her meager gift would offer any kind of comfort for all of this? A small framed color-pencil sketch of his wife and daughter as birds, birds in repose and not even in flight, birds with human faces and legs, a life study of dead models. Drawn against an umber-and-red background, the wife was an

Antillean mango bird with iridescent purple tail feathers and emerald-green wings; and the daughter, a ruby-throated hummingbird with a gilded body.

The package was on a side table near her sofa. She walked over, picked it up, and handed it to him. She thought, as he unwrapped the plain brown paper, that it seemed like it might be meant for an ancestral shrine. Looking down at it, he tipped his head to the side as if to confirm what he was seeing. Then his mouth fell open as it sank in.

"What is this?" he asked.

"An expression of regret," she said.

She now realized that not just giving him the sketch, but her making it at all, was confusing to him. This had not been her intention. She wanted it to be a kind of memorial to his wife and daughter. But it was too soon.

He held out his hands and pulled her closer so that the two of them could see the drawing from the same angle.

"You know this is some crazy shit, right?" he said.

She had to admit that both the intent and execution were crazy as hell. Perhaps he wasn't the only one who needed to be in a psychiatric hospital. She looked up at the side of his face, and he seemed to be trying hard to suppress a laugh.

"If you want to do something for me, draw me a picture where you make them look older," he said once he was fully composed. "Like when kids are lost for a long time and the police make them look older."

He was talking about image enhancement, age progression. She spent the last day of her class at Miami Dade discussing forensics and courtroom sketching as possible career choices for her student artists. Even though she'd never done them professionally, she had once shown him how she could sketch anyone at both present and older ages, without even looking down at the paper. She was going to tell him that he could get software to do what he wanted to see—he could upload some pictures on his computer and add as many years as he'd like. But then she thought how soothing it might feel to age progress his daughter, to do away with the baby fat, sharpen the jawline, lengthen the neck, stretch her whole body for height, and later give her buds for breasts. Then to gift his

wife with a few more years. To add gray strands
to her hair, crow's-feet around her eyes, to round
out her shoulders and fill out her middle.

"You don't have to do it now," he said, his
eyes still fixed on their bird faces. "I might ask
in a year or two. Or even later than that."

Was this his way of telling her they might still
be in each other's lives in two or three years?

"I have to go," he said, handing the frame to
her. "Thank you for this evening."

She put the sketch back on the side table
where it had been since she'd wrapped it that
afternoon, then followed him to the door. She
opened it for him and gripped the handle as he
prepared to walk through. Before he could step
off her threshold, she asked, "Did your wife
know about me?"

He turned around to face her again
and nodded.

"You told her?"

"She saw us," he said. "At the restaurant that
last night. She figured out that I was hanging
out there a lot. She came to see what was up."

She now felt an extra layer of shame. She was
also impressed that his wife did not confront
them or cause a scene.

"The trip to Haiti was about setting things

straight with her," he said. "We were going to work on our marriage while surrounded by family. Having family around always made us feel more tied together."

"You were working things out with Dina?" she said.

Dina's name coming across Anika's lips seemed to startle him, as though he wasn't aware that Anika even knew it.

She thought just then of telling him about their baby, but she decided not to. It would just mean more grief for him to carry, another loss. Or perhaps he would be relieved that he wouldn't have to be a father again, or be linked to another woman through a child.

He turned his back to her, and with his neck curved as if to bow, he walked down the hall. He made up for the slight imbalance in the prosthetic leg by bouncing too hard in the other direction, which made him seem unsteady in a way that she had not noticed when he'd arrived for dinner. Watching him stagger into the elevator, she wondered how he was managing all this alone. But then she reminded herself that he had been living without her for months now.

After the elevator doors closed, and the possibility of his returning diminished, she walked back inside her apartment. She looked for and found the old Pinot Noir bottle in one of her kitchen cabinets and brought it out with her, along with the sketch, to the terrace.

She placed the sketch of the bird versions of Qadine and Dina on one of her patio chairs, and while sitting next to them, she looked down at the causeway and at the long line of cars slowly making their way across it, cars filled with couples, families returning from barbecues and fireworks displays.

"You two must look after each other," she said to the drawing.

She wanted them to look after her child, too. Her child would also never age. Her child would never even be visible to the eye. She wanted all three of them, Qadine, Dina, and her too-early-to-be-named baby, to take in the same reflection of the downtown skyline she was seeing. She wanted them, her angels of history, to collectively admire this liquid city on the bay.

She uncorked the wine, threw her head back, and took a swig from the bottle. The wine tasted like fizzy vinegar. It seared her tongue, then singed her throat as she forced herself to swallow. It was undrinkable. She thought of Roro and his rum pouring and emptied the rest of the bottle on her terrace's cement floor. It was so rancid that she expected it to look like de-oxygenated blood, but instead it looked mostly brown, like melted skin.

As she watched the wine thin out and spread around her feet, she whispered, just as she had with Roro and the others the night of the earth-quake, "Pou sa n pa wè yo. For those we don't see. For those who are not here."

Hot-Air Balloons

My roommate Neah dropped out of college the first semester of her first year to work full-time for Leve, a women's organization that runs, among other things, a rape recovery center in a poor neighborhood in Port-au-Prince. After her one-week Thanksgiving trip to Haiti with Leve, Neah sent a group e-mail, in which both her parents and I and a few of her professors were included, telling us that she was back in Miami but would not be returning to school.

Neah's father was Dr. Frank Asher, the esteemed Trinidadian linguistic anthropologist and chair of the Caribbean Studies Department. He was a lean, baby-faced man with ruddy cheeks and freckles. In fact, he looked a lot like Neah with her pointy cheekbones and tawny-colored skin, which sometimes seemed to disappear, along with Neah, under her loose-fitting, dark thrift-shop pants and marching-band-inspired jackets. If not for the fragile-looking wire-rimmed glasses that Neah said she couldn't convince him to replace, and a signature plaid sports coat that Neah called his old-man blazer, Dr. Asher would look like the son of most of his colleagues. In fact, he was younger than a lot of them. He and Neah's mother, an economist, had gotten married during their first year in graduate school. Neah came early in the marriage and was, she believed, the reason for her parents' divorce. Still, when Dr. Asher suggested that she decline admission to, among others, the college where her mother was teaching in upstate New York, in the small town where Neah had mostly grown up, to attend the college in Miami where her father was a big shot, Neah decided to give it a try.

Dr. Asher was now sitting on Neah's bed, quietly rubbing his forehead as if waiting for her to walk through the door. Neah's dropping-out e-mail had disturbed him enough to make him rush over to our room and talk to me in person, but he wasn't doing much talking.

Neah's and my room was larger than most of the other rooms on our first-year floor, with two twin beds instead of three, a shared closet, and individual dressers on opposite ends. Next to each of our beds was a desk with a bookshelf on top. Among my opened books and notebooks, and snack wrappers, was a framed picture of me and my parents, which they had insisted we have taken at a strip mall a week before move-in day. I kept that picture on my desk so I would always think about my parents when I sat down to do my work. Seeing the three of us, my dad in his charcoal-gray suit, my mom in a pink ruffled dress, and me with a flowered maxi, all of us with our heart-shaped faces glowing with smiles, always reminded me that I couldn't afford to fail.

Neah had no pictures or posters on her side of the room. She thought print pictures were old school. The faces of everyone she treasured, including her friends, parents, and other family members from New York, were on her phone. Aside from my family photo, I had no other pictures on display. I found the blank white walls soothing to look at when I was sad, tired, or just daydreaming. Unlike most of our floor mates, we didn't have a small refrigerator or microwave in our room. Neah was vehemently anticlutter, and I was used to keeping only as many belongings as I could quickly pack up and take with me.

Neah's bed was well made, with hospital corners and fluffed pillows, just as she had left it the morning Dr. Asher had driven her to the airport for the trip to Port-au-Prince a week ago. The books Neah left behind were neatly lined up on her desk. Dr. Asher picked up and leafed through several of them. He lingered on a book of poetry called **Illuminations,** in which he stopped to silently read some pages.

Right before she left, Neah had been immersed in the work of the French poet Arthur Rimbaud, which she pronounced "Rambo." She told me she was "overjoyed" with the possibilities that a few of his poems had opened up to her. She was planning to enroll in more French classes in the spring so that she could bypass translations and read Rimbaud in the original. She said she was going to spend her junior year in Paris and eventually get a PhD in French literature and write her dissertation on the symbolists with Rimbaud as her focus.

"Lucy," said Dr. Asher. "You hold some responsibility for all of this." He closed **Illuminations** but still held on to it. His voice was clear, resolute, and well paced, the way I imagined him speaking to his students in class. "Can you please go to that place and talk to my daughter about returning to school? She is not answering my calls."

Neah learned about Leve, the women's organization, from me. My twenty-hour-a-week work-study job was in Career/Volunteer Services, and one of the first things I saw there on a bulletin board was a flyer with the Leve logo, a silhouette of a woman and a young girl staring up at a dark sky with a single star in it. On the flyer were color photographs of undernourished Haitian women who looked like my mother, some carrying heavy buckets of water on their heads while walking narrow dirt paths in the countryside, others sitting on riverbanks washing clothes, a few selling fly-covered meat in an open market. At the bottom of the flyer, near the pitch to join Leve on the Thanksgiving-week trip, was a picture of a teenage girl lying in a hospital bed, her face bruised, her eyes swollen shut.

I waited until no one was looking and yanked the flyer off the bulletin board, in part because I was afraid that people would link that girl's bruised face to mine, as someone who, though I was not born there, considered myself "left side of the hyphen" Haitian. Where were the idyllic beaches with fine white sand that my parents were always dreaming and talking about, and that I had also seen online? Where were the dewy mountaintops, Haiti being the land of mountains and all? Where was the Citadelle Laferrière, one of the world's greatest forts? Where were the caves and grottoes, the waterfalls, the cathedrals, churches, Vodou temples, museums, and art galleries college students could be visiting?

That night, I had described both the flyer and my indignation to Neah. She was so quiet I thought she had fallen asleep. After a long pause, she said in her late-night-whisper voice, "It sounds really interesting. I think I'd like to go."

"I would not want to go," I said. I meant without my parents, but I never managed to say that.

It didn't surprise me that Neah would want to go on the Leve trip, though. She had traveled all over the world with her parents, even after their divorce.

I had grown up differently than Neah. My parents met while traveling between orange, berries, lettuce, tomatoes, and corn harvests along the Georgia and Florida coasts. For as far back as I could remember, I had slept in grower-owned housing, which was basically bunk beds and sometimes cots behind barns and stables, where only thin wooden slats and planks separated my parents and me from the animals. We'd also lived in field barracks with beaten-dirt floors, in "dorms" that looked like they'd been built for criminals doing hard labor, and in overpriced motel rooms with cracked windows, filthy carpets, and peeling paint on the walls.

Every time we moved to a new place, my parents would enroll me in a new school. I would spend a few weeks settling in, make a friend or two, then have to move again. Many of the older kids who were in school with me would eventually drop out and start working in the fields with their parents to make money, but my parents wouldn't let me. The fields were for them and not for me, my father said. Me coming to work in the fields with them would be like them washing their hands and drying them in the dirt, my mother said.

Every night after work, my father would check my homework, which he pretended to understand even when he didn't. I was ordered daily by my mother to study hard and make something of myself so I wouldn't turn out to be a teenage mom or a farmworker. My dream was always to have a stable home and to stay in one place.

The place that felt most like home, and where my parents kept returning for the summer harvests, was a trailer park in Belle Glade, Florida, where, when we were lucky, we could rent a two-room trailer away from the hot and noisy parking lot and near a canal in the back, where you could smell the earthy scent of the soil, rather than the pong of the concrete when it rained. It was in Belle Glade that I attended, every summer, a six-week program for migrant kids, a kind of educational camp, which made up for all that I missed while constantly changing schools so that my parents could chase harvests, sometimes four or five times a year. The summer camp showed the hundred or so of us kids who participated in it that plants could be grown to just be beautiful in the botanical gardens we visited, and that some people owned old and new things that they displayed in museums and galleries. I learned to swim in the pool at the high school where the program was based. We went to concerts and plays. We were taught how to take tests and were encouraged to dream of going to college.

I remember hearing Neah sniffle in the dark when I told her all this during the first day of orientation week and our first night together in our room.

"See, we were not randomly matched after all," she said, once she'd collected herself. "Academics' kids are migrants of a different kind."

"Neah will be fine," I told Dr. Asher before he left our room with her copy of **Illuminations** that night. "I will go find her and talk to her."

Unlike the Haitian restaurant and barbershop next door, which blasted lively konpa and rasin music from giant speakers into the street and had people walking in and out of them, the glass-fronted Leve office in Little Haiti was quiet. The walls, which were completely visible from the street, were covered with more photographs of sad, but also many hopeful-looking, women, their eyes aimed like laser beams at the camera. I could see Neah and another woman in profile as they worked at their desks across from each other. Even in the eighty-degree-plus heat, Neah was wearing a thick brown jacket that looked like it was older than she was. She had probably picked it up from one of the Salvation Armies and Goodwills that provided most of our wardrobe, me out of necessity and her out of choice. Her face was gaunter now than when I had last seen her more than a week ago. She was stooped over, her back at a sharp and uncomfortable-looking angle.

I watched her all morning from a wobbly table outside the coffee shop across the street. She kept staring at her computer screen. Finally, she got up from behind the desk, walked over to the other woman's corner, and exchanged a few words with her. She then strolled out onto the street, where she pulled a cigarette from her jacket pocket and cupped her hands around her mouth to light up. I didn't realize she was a smoker, but then again, she might have been secretly smoking without me knowing it.

I finished my coffee, then crossed the busy street. I was still hoping I could make our meeting seem accidental.

"Hey Né," I said, when she looked up and saw me.

"Hey," she said while absentmindedly stroking her flat chest.

She seemed to be expecting me. She opened

one of her palms, spat in it, put out the cigarette with her spit, then put the wet stub in her
jacket pocket.

"I see you got my e-mail," she said.

"So you went on the Thanksgiving-break trip
and now this is all you want to do with your
life?" I asked.

She looked back at the office and sighed. She
had left one of the drawers in her desk open,
and she seemed torn between going back in to
close it and standing there talking to me.

"How are you?" I asked.

She turned her face away from me, and I followed her gaze to a fox terrier, which was sleeping while tied to a parking meter in front of the
coffee shop across the street. The fox terrier was
mostly white, with black patches. Or at least I
thought Neah was watching the terrier.

I remembered telling her during one of our
late-night chats how the summer I turned fif-
teen, I convinced my parents to let me get a
learner's permit. My dad bought an old station
wagon with over two hundred thousand miles
on it and taught me to drive.

One Sunday afternoon, I was driving on the
edge of one of Muck City's many cane fields
with my father in the passenger seat and my

mother in the back. We were approaching a row of shotgun houses on the side of a canal when a liver-colored pit bull came out of nowhere and ran in front of the car. The car windows were down because the car had no air-conditioning.

When I hit the dog, I heard the crash, a long whimper, then a pleading moan as both the car's front and back wheels ran over it. I stopped and looked out through the side mirrors. The dog's body was still and looked crushed, but I didn't see any blood, which maybe was hidden by the coat. I knew it was a pit bull because a few of our neighbors in the trailer park had them. A couple of the boys from the summer program had their pit bulls fight in the cane fields. I never had the heart to go watch, but a bunch of the other girls went and bet on those fights.

My father panicked and told me to press on the gas.

"We can't leave it here," I said.

"What will you do with a dead dog?" my mother asked.

The car stalled as I hesitated. My father got out and raced to the driver's seat. I started crying as I jumped into the passenger seat before my father sped away.

"We could have taken it to a vet," I said.

"Stop being stupid," my mother answered. "You have that kind of money? Besides, it will die soon, if it's lucky. Who knows what the owners would do to us, if they find us. If we're killed because of that dog, there will be no one to cry over us."

I remembered telling Neah one night how I was never able to look at dogs again, any dogs at all, without thinking of that day, or could never watch my parents make a quick collective decision without thinking of death, which is why, right before classes started, I had the image of a small, brown, living pit bull tattooed on the inside of my right wrist, on the hand I'd kept on the wheel as that dog died. Neah looked down at my tattoo, reached over, and stroked it gently.

"Come and have a coffee with me," she said, "even though you've already had some."

"You saw me sitting there and you didn't come out?"

"You came for me." She turned back for a moment to look at the open drawer and at the other woman in the office who was also watching us. The woman looked older, though not old enough to be, say, my mother. She was wearing a red sleeveless jumper and had her hair in two large cornrows with white thread woven through them. This, along with her bright red fingernail polish, made her seem overly glamorous for her line of work. Holding up one index finger, Neah pointed at me, then at the coffee shop. The woman nodded her approval.

I felt like holding Neah's hand protectively, the way one might hold a small child's hand, to cross the street, and I would have, I think, if she wasn't walking a whole lot faster than me. Neither one of us stopped when we passed the sleeping terrier.

I followed Neah to a table in the back of the coffee shop, near the bathrooms. The air was cooler there than it was outside, but it was also much darker in that spot than in the rest of the place, which was filling up slowly with lunchtime customers. The waiter came over and, though he recognized me from earlier, seemed annoyed when we ordered only two cups of hot chocolate and none of the panini and sandwiches and desserts he kept recommending to us.

Sitting there, I felt as though our time together had no limit, like we might be sipping our hot chocolates forever. But just as I had seen her do in the past when she was trying to figure out what to say, Neah began rubbing her cheeks so hard that I was worried she might buff them down to the bone.

"The trip was awful, Luce," she blurted out. "It wasn't the trip itself that was awful. It was the circumstances."

"How so?" I asked.

"Remember that class we dropped where they tried to teach us how to draw without looking down at the paper?"

Blind Contour Drawing was the only class we had attempted to take together. Even though it did not result in either one of us making more friends, we had tried to branch out on our own, even choosing different mandatory first-year seminars, hers leading her to Rimbaud, and mine to Taino mythology.

"This trip was blind-contour everything," she said while still rubbing her cheeks. "I had no idea what I was getting into at the rape recovery clinic."

"I'm sorry." I reached over and pulled her hands away from her face. She looked down at them as though she wasn't sure what to do, then she raised her body up a bit and sat on them, all while avoiding my eyes.

"I saw all kinds of things you wouldn't believe. I saw women who'd had their tongues bitten off by the men who raped them," she said.

She spent most of her week there with teenage girls, some as young as thirteen and fourteen, with fistulas as wide as the top of the cups we were drinking from, girls with syphilis scars running down their legs. She met a few girls who'd been working street corners in badly lit areas, where they were gang-raped by clients, and others who'd been recruited for orgies with international aid workers, trading sex for food, then realizing that they had no control over how much sex or food they were there for.

I was the one who was now avoiding her eyes. I couldn't even look at the cups on the table in front of us.

"I can understand now why you didn't want to go on that trip," she said.

But she wasn't entirely right. My not wanting to go with her was both simple and complicated. First of all, you had to pay for the airfare yourself, and I didn't have the money. Neah's father had paid for her airfare. She had offered to get him to pay for mine, but I was too proud to accept. And yes, I did not want to see any of the stuff she was talking about on my first trip there. I first wanted to see the beaches, the mountains, the citadel, the waterfalls, the cathedrals, the museums of Haiti. I also hated being constantly reminded that I was lucky to **not** be among those women that groups like Leve were helping. I hated that their help was needed in the first place.

Neah had seen hopeful things, too. Along with counseling, therapy, and meditation, older Haitian neighborhood women comforted the girls with storytelling and song. Others came to teach self-defense classes. Not speaking Creole, Neah mostly held the girls while vowing in a phrase that the Haiti-based Leve women had taught her—m pap janm bliye nou—that she would never forget them.

When she came back to Miami, she had a symbol of her commitment tattooed on her chest at the same tattoo parlor, a few miles off campus, where I'd had the pit bull tattooed on my wrist. Her tattoo, she said, was on her chest bone, near her heart. I was afraid to ask what the tattoo was of, but soon I didn't have to.

One morning, she explained, she woke up in the rape recovery center, where she was also staying, and in an open window frame saw two clear plastic bags filled with water. The residents had strung them to the windows to keep out the flies. The flies and their many eyes saw—it was believed—magnified, giant, monstrously distorted versions of themselves in the water-filled plastic bags and fled.

"How do you tattoo that on your chest?" I asked.

"The same way you tattoo a dog on your wrist," she said, "but I had someone incompetent do it, and my tattoos don't look like water bags, but two hot-air balloons."

"Can I see?" I asked.

"No," she said. "It is not for viewing. It's private."

Even as she said this, she smiled, which meant that she might eventually let me see her tattoo after all.

"What do you do in there?" I asked, pointing in the general direction of her desk across the street.

"I'm not an official employee," she said. "Not really on the books. They don't have the funds for it, but they—and 'they' is mostly Josette—she lets me write grants and donation-request e-mails and letters."

"Are you going to move in with your dad now?" I asked.

"I'm staying with Josette right now, but my mom is going to help out," she said.

"So your mom's okay with what you're doing?"

"She thought I needed a gap year anyway, but Dad insisted I start right away."

Obviously tired of the subject, she added, "I better get back to work."

She got up from the table and started walking toward the door. I had no choice but to follow her, and as we reached the doorway, I slipped in next to her and let my fingers brush against hers before she moved ahead.

Outside, the terrier at the parking meter was gone. Standing where it had been, Neah said, "My parents would call my saying this redundant, but, Luce, there's so much suffering in the world."

The type of music being blasted from the record store across the street had changed. A Creole gospel song was now blaring from the speakers.

"Can I come see you again?" I asked.

"Sure," she said, then began walking across the street.

She was nearly halfway to the curb when a car screeched to a halt and the driver honked loudly because she was walking too slowly.

Looking lost, as though the man peeking his head out the car window shouting obscenities at her was an apparition in a strange dream, she walked back to the parking meter, where I was standing. Leaning in, she looked at me with the same intense sadness I was feeling, while longing to both yell at her for being careless and pull her into my arms to celebrate the fact that she was okay.

I thought she was about to walk away when she pivoted and raised her arms, as if reaching for something above me. Her fingers landed on my back, shaking. She smelled like chocolates and cigarettes. She leaned over, buried her face in my neck, and hugged me. I felt as though she was trying to squeeze into me everything she was feeling, everything she had ever felt. I tried to keep us linked for as long as I could, clutching and clinging to her back, but then she gently drove her palms against my chest and pushed me away.

Suddenly the rest of the world was there again, the cars and the waiter, with the bill we had not paid.

"I got this," I told both her and the waiter.

I paid the waiter with part of the hundred dollars my parents were still wiring me every week in spite of my scholarship and work-study pay. Neah crossed the street, walked back to the Leve office, and sat down at her desk. She turned her chair away from the street and started a conversation with Josette. Josette smiled at something she said, but I couldn't see Neah's face and couldn't tell whether she was smiling or not. After their brief chat, she and Josette went back to reading their e-mails and making their phone calls. The wobbly table where I'd spent most of the morning opened up, and I went back to sitting there, on the sidewalk, outside the coffee shop. I kept waiting for Neah to look my way, but she never did, not even when I got up and left.

That night, Dr. Asher came back to the room to pick up some of Neah's things. I supposed he'd gone to see her, too, and she'd convinced him that working for Leve was the best thing for her.

"She looked good," I said, keeping to my side of the room as he moved around briskly packing some of her clothes and books into a large duffel bag he'd brought with him. I wasn't sure what he was taking with him and what he was leaving behind, and I did not want to get in his way.

"She seemed fine." He stopped and slid his hands over the bright yellow sheets on her bed, but left them in place.

I wanted to tell him how much I'd enjoyed that Friday night Neah had invited me to have dinner with the two of them at his off-campus apartment, before she left for Haiti. I wanted to tell him how I had also slid my hand over the tan brown leather sofa in his living room, the one whose seats and back cushions felt softer than my own skin. I wanted to tell him how I also stroked the spines of his books while trying to memorize the titles, even though his wall-to-wall bookshelves looked like wallpaper to me. I wanted to tell him that though I did not understand most of the art in his bedroom and guest room and the paintings he insisted on having Neah show me, I liked that they looked like spilled paint and ice-cream swirls, and even mistakes. I wanted him to know that I also liked the wooden and bronze African masks in his home office and the black-and-white and color photographs in his bathroom and kitchen, especially the ones filled with sunsets and outdoor marketplaces from all over the world.

His goat roti and corn soup were already cooked by the time we'd arrived at his place. He had asked Neah and me to make a salad, and while we were gathering the ingredients from his fridge, Neah told him that she'd started reading Rimbaud.

"That's my girl," he'd casually said, as if he had been hearing about her extraordinary interests and discoveries all her life.

"What's your favorite so far?" he'd asked.

"I'm digging **Illuminations,**" she'd said.

"I'm a Baudelaire man myself," he said. Then they'd both looked over at me twirling the salad spinner, and before I could feel too excluded, they'd changed the subject to something like which dressing would be best.

"Take care of yourself, Lucy," Dr. Asher said as he walked out of our room with some of Neah's things in the duffel bag.

"I will," I said.

"Don't be a stranger," he added.

That same night, I was nearly asleep when I heard the door crack open. I sat up on my bed, alarmed that it might be someone breaking in. It was Neah. She was standing in the doorway with a halo of light from the hallway encircling her. She was still in the same clothes she'd been wearing that morning.

She closed the door, and as she walked toward her bed in the dark, I heard her pulling a bag behind her. She turned on her desk lamp, and I blinked, forcing my eyes to adjust to its glare.

I said, "Né."

She said, "Hey."

"What are you doing here?"

"I'm staying," she said, not exactly sounding thrilled about it.

She walked over to her dresser and picked up her shower caddy, then pulled a towel and one of those wide white T-shirts she slept in from the top drawer of her dresser.

"You changed your mind?" I asked.

"I did," she said.

I wondered if it was me or her father who'd convinced her to come back.

"Josette wouldn't let me stay unless I finished the semester," she said.

Her father had probably talked to Josette.

"I'm still going to volunteer there," she said, before walking out of the room.

She was in the shower for what seemed like a longer time than usual. I listened for signs of her in the hall and followed the thump of footsteps walking to and from the rooms to the showers and kitchen area until she returned.

She was wearing the oversize T-shirt when she came back. Without saying anything, she put the shower caddy, her clothes, and her towel on top of her dresser. She then turned off her desk light and slipped into bed.

"I'm glad you're back," I said, hoping she would not fall asleep too quickly.

"I'm too easily swayed by stories," she said, her voice already fading into the dark.

"What do you mean?" I asked. This sounded like something her father might have told her to convince her to come back to school.

"I am too easily swayed by every story I hear, or see, or witness, especially the tragic ones," she said. "I think this is going to be the story of my life. I'm going to be the girl who is too easily swayed by other people's stories."

"I think you're going to be the girl who helps other people," I said. "A Mother Teresa type."

"I hear she slept on rags on the floor of some Ritz-Carlton sometimes," she said.

"And then she went out and tried to save the world," I said.

"And what kind of girl are you?" she asked.

I didn't have to think too much about this. I already knew. I am the girl—the woman—who is always going to be looking for stability, a safe harbor. I am never going to forget that I can easily lose everything I have, including my life, in one instant. But this is not what I told her. I told her that I was going to be the kind of friend she could always count on, the kind of friend who might even go on a Leve trip with her.

She said nothing, and I realized that she had fallen asleep. I heard the hum of the light snoring that signaled her deepest sleep. Though it had sometimes annoyed me, I was happy to hear it again.

When the snore was at its peak and I knew it would take a freight train to wake her, I turned on my desk lamp and walked over to her side of the room. She was lying on her back, which is probably what led to her snoring in the first place. Her shirt was so large and so loose that it was easy to lower the neckline without touching her skin.

I moved the fabric down toward her small breasts, and there it was, on her breastbone, two quarter-sized hot-air balloons without the baskets, one balloon indigo blue, and the other bloodred, two versions of the colors of the Haitian flag. Underneath the balloons, where the baskets would have been, and written in cursive, in red ink, were the words JE EST UN

AUTRE. This is what she'd been writing her paper on before leaving for Haiti. Rimbaud's "I is another."

Because my parents were working a new harvest route in Mississippi and would not have much time off for Thanksgiving while Neah was in Haiti, I stayed on campus, ate a Thanksgiving meal with the foreign students in the dining hall, and read about Tainos for my first-year seminar class.

The Tainos believed themselves to have originally been cave people who would turn into stone when touched by sunlight. They knew the risk when they stepped into the light, but they did it anyway in order to create a new world, a world that continues to exist, because we are still here. I thought that the next time we were chatting while half-asleep, I might tell Neah that story. In the meantime, while she was still asleep, I lowered my right wrist to the crevice between her breasts and let it rest there for a moment. And briefly, very briefly, my pain and hers embraced.

Sunrise, Sunset

1

It comes on again on her grandson's christening day. A lost moment, a blank spot, one that Carole does not know how to measure. She is there one second, then she is not. She knows exactly where she is, then she does not. Her older church friends tell similar stories about their surgeries, how they count backward from ten with an oxygen mask over their faces, then wake up before reaching one, only to find that hours, and sometimes even days, have gone by. She feels as though she were experiencing the same thing.

Her son-in-law, James, a dreadlocked high-school math teacher, is holding her grandson, Jude, who has inherited her daughter's globe-shaped head, penny-colored skin, and long fingers, which he wraps around Carole's chin whenever she holds him. Jude is a lively giggler. His whole body shakes when he laughs. Carole often stares at him for hours, hoping that his chubby face will bring back memories of her own children at that age, memories that are quickly slipping away.

Her daughter, Jeanne, is still about sixty pounds overweight on Jude's christening day, seven months after his birth. Jeanne is so miserable about this—and who knows what else—that she spends most days in her bedroom, hiding. Since her daughter is stuck in a state of mental fragility, Carole welcomes the opportunity to join Jude's other grandmother, Grace, in watching their grandson as often as she's asked. Carole likes to entertain Jude with whatever children's songs and peekaboo games she can still remember, including one she calls Solèy Leve, Solèy Kouche—Sunrise, Sunset—which she used to play with her children. She drapes a black sheet over her grandson's playpen and pronounces it sunset, then takes the sheet off and calls it sunrise. Her grandson does not seem to mind when she gets confused and reverses the order. He doesn't know the difference anyway.

Sometimes Carole forgets who Grace is and

mistakes her for the nanny. She does, however, remember that Grace disapproved of her son's marrying Jeanne, whom she believed was beneath him. That censure now seems justified by Jeanne's failures as a mother.

Jeanne, Carole thinks, has never known real tragedy. Growing up in a country ruled by a merciless dictator, Carole watched her neighbors being dragged out of their houses by the dictator's denim-uniformed henchmen. One of her aunts was beaten almost to death for throwing herself in front of her husband as he was being arrested. Carole's father left the country for Cuba when she was twelve and never returned. Her mother's only means of survival was cleaning the houses of people who were barely able to pay her.

Carole's best friend lived next door, in another tin-roofed room, rented separately from the same landlord. During the night, while her mother slept, Carole often heard her friend being screamed at by her own mother, who seemed to hate her for being alive. Carole tried so hard to protect her US-born children from these stories that they are now incapable of overcoming any kind of sadness. Not so much her son, Paul, who is a minister, but Jeanne, whom she named after her childhood friend. Her daughter's psyche is so feeble that anything can rattle her. Doesn't she realize that the life she is living is an accident of fortune? Doesn't she know that she is an exception in this world, where it is normal to be unhappy, to be hungry, to work nonstop and earn next to nothing, and to suffer the whims of everything from tyrants to hurricanes and earthquakes?

The morning of her grandson's christening, Carole is wearing a long-sleeved white lace dress that she can't recall putting on. She has combed her hair back in a tight bun that now hurts a little. Earlier in the week, she watched from the terrace of her daughter's third-floor apartment as Jeanne dipped her feet in the condo's kidney-shaped communal pool. She'd walked out onto the terrace to look at the water, the unusual cobalt-blue color it becomes in late afternoon and the slow ripple of its surface, even when untouched by a breeze or bodies.

"I won't christen him!" Jeanne was shouting on the phone. "That's her thing, not ours."

"We're up soon," James says, snapping Carole out of her reverie. He is using the tone of voice with which he speaks to Jude. It's clear that this is not the first time he's told her this. Her daughter is looking neither at her nor at the congregation full of Carole's friends. She's not even looking at Jude, who has been dressed, most likely by James, in a plain white romper. Jeanne stares at the floor as others take turns holding Jude and keeping him quiet in the church: first Grace, then Carole's husband, Victor; then James's younger sister, Zoe, who is the godmother; then James's best friend, Marcos, the godfather.

Carole keeps reminding herself that her daughter is still young. Only thirty-two. Jeanne was once a satisfied young woman, a guidance counselor at the school where James teaches. (When James and Jeanne first started dating, their friends called them J.J.; then Jude was born, and the three of them became Triple J.)

"She used to like children, right?" Carole sometimes asks Victor. "Before she had her son?"

When Jude's name is called from the pulpit by his uncle Paul, James motions for them to approach the altar. Paul, dressed in a long white ministerial robe, steps down from the pulpit and, while Jude is still in his father's arms, traces a cross on his forehead with scented oil. The oil bothers Jude's eyes, and he wails. Undeterred, Paul takes Jude and begins praying so loudly that he shocks Jude into silence. After the prayer, he hands Jude back to his mother. Jeanne kisses her son's oil-soaked forehead, and her eyes balloon with tears.

Carole knows that her daughter is not enjoying any of this, but Carole has found comfort in such rituals, and she believes that her grandson will not be protected against the world's evils—including his mother's lack of interest in him—until this one is performed.

Later, at the post-christening lunch at her daughter's apartment, Carole spots James and Jeanne walking out of their bedroom. Jude is in Jeanne's arms. They have changed the boy out of his plain romper into an even-plainer sleeveless onesie. Jeanne stops in the doorway and raises a bib over Jude's face and murmurs, "Sunset." Then she lowers the bib and squeals, "Sunrise!"

Watching her daughter play this game with the baby, Carole feels as though she herself were going through the motions, raising and lowering the bib. Not at this very moment but at some point in the hazy past. It's as if Jeanne has become Carole, and James has become her once-dapper and lanky husband, Victor, who now walks with a cane that he is always tapping against the ground.

All is not lost, Carole thinks. Her daughter has learned a few things from her, after all. Then it returns again, that all-too-familiar sensation of herself waning. What if she never recognizes anyone again? What if she forgets her husband? What if she stops remembering what it's like to love him, a feeling that has changed so much over the years, in ways that her daughter's love for her own husband seems also to be changing, even though James, like Victor, is patient. She's never seen him shout at or scold Jeanne. He doesn't even tell her to get out of bed or pay more attention to their child. He tells Carole and his own mother that Jeanne just needs time. But how long will this kind of tolerance last? How long can anyone bear to live with someone whose mind wanders off to a place where their love no longer exists?

Carole's husband is the only one who knows how far along she is. He is constantly subjected to her sudden mood changes, her bursts of anger followed by total stillness. He has tried for years to help her hide her symptoms, or lessen them with puzzles and other educational games, with coconut oil and omega-3 supplements, which she takes with special juices and teas. He is always turning off appliances, finding keys she's stored in unusual places like the oven or the freezer. He helps her finish sentences, nudges her to let her know if she has repeated something a few times. But one day he will grow tired of this and put her in a home, where strangers will have to take care of her.

When Jude was born, Victor bought her a doll so that she could practice taking care of their grandson. It's a brown boy doll with a round face and tight peppercorn curls, like Jude's. When she puts the doll in the bath, its hair clings to its scalp, just like Jude's. Bathing the doll, then dressing it before bed, makes her feel calm, helps her sleep more soundly. But this, like her illness, is still a secret between her husband and her, a secret that they may not be able to keep much longer.

2

How do you become a good mother? Jeanne wants to ask someone, anyone. She wishes she'd been brave enough to ask her mother before her dementia, or whatever it is that she is suffering from, set in. Her mother refuses to have tests done and get a definitive diagnosis, and her father is fine with that.

"You don't poke around for something you don't want to find," he's told Jeanne a few times.

Her father offers the first toast at the christening lunch. "To Jude, who brought us together today," he says in Creole, then in English.

James hands Jeanne a Champagne glass, which she has trouble balancing while holding their son. Her mother puts her own glass down and reaches over and takes Jude from Jeanne's arms.

"I'll toast with him," Carole says, and Jeanne fears her mother may actually believe that Jude's body is a Champagne glass. She is afraid these days to let her mother hold her son, to leave them alone together, but since she and James are close by and Jude isn't fussing or fidgeting, she does not protest.

After the toast, James asks if he can get Jeanne and her mother a plate of food. Carole nods, then quickly changes her mind. "Maybe later," she says. Jude is looking up at her now, his baby eyes fixed on her wrinkled and weary-looking face.

Carole isn't eating much these days. Jeanne, on the other hand, feels as though a deep and sour hole were burrowing through her body, an abyss that is always demanding to be filled. James doesn't insist on anything, including that she get out of bed when she's spent several days and nights just lying there. It's not his style. Throughout their courtship and marriage, he's never pressured her to do anything. Everything is always presented to her as a suggestion or a recommendation. It's as if he were constantly practicing being patient for the rowdy kids he teaches at school. Even there, he never loses his temper. Her mother, on the other hand, has been lashing out lately, though afterward she seems unable to remember doing it. She has always been a quiet woman. She is certainly kinder than James's mother, who wouldn't have given Jeanne or Carole the time of day if it weren't for James.

Jeanne often wonders if her mother was happier in Haiti. She doubts it. Jeanne has no right to be sad, her mother has often told her. Only Carole has the right to be sad, because she has seen and heard terrible things. Jeanne's father's approach to life is different. He is more interested than anybody Jeanne knows in the pleasure of joy, or the joy of pleasure, however you want to put it. It's as if he had sworn to enjoy every second of his life—to wear the best

clothes he can afford, to eat the best food, to
go to dances where his favorite Haitian bands
are playing.

Victor drove a city bus for most of Jeanne's
childhood, then when he got older he switched
to driving a taxicab. Between fares, he sat in
the parking lot at Miami International Airport,
discussing Haitian politics with his cabdriver
friends. Perhaps her mother wouldn't be losing
her mind if she'd worked outside their home.
Church committees and family were her life's
work, a luxury they'd been able to afford because Victor worked double shifts and took
extra weekend jobs. Carole could have worked,
if she'd wanted to, as a lunch lady in a school
cafeteria or as an elder companion or a nanny,
like many of her church friends.

Jeanne never wanted to be a housewife like
her mother, but here she is now, stuck at home
with her son. She doesn't leave the house much
anymore, except for her son's doctor's appoint-
ments. Most of the time, she's afraid to leave
her bed, afraid even to hold her son, for fear
that she might drop him or hug him too tightly
and smother him. Then the fatigue sets in, an
exhaustion so forceful it doesn't even allow her
to sleep. Motherhood is a kind of foggy bubble

she can't step out of long enough to wrap her arms around her child. Oddly enough, he's an easy child. He's been sleeping through the night since the day they brought him home. He naps regularly. He isn't colicky or difficult. He is just there.

James decides to offer a toast of his own. He taps his Champagne glass with a spoon to catch everyone's attention.

"I want to make a toast to my wife, not only for being a phenomenal wife and mother but for bravely bringing Jude into our lives," he says.

Why does he want to think of her as brave? Perhaps he's thinking of the twenty-six hours of labor that ended in a C-section, during which her son was pulled out with the umbilical cord wrapped around his neck. He had nearly died, the doctor told her, because of her stubborn insistence on a natural birth.

The pregnancy had been easy. She'd worked a regular schedule until the day she went into labor. The pain was intense, pulsating, throbbing, but bearable, even after the twenty-fifth hour. First babies can put you through the wringer, the nurses kept telling her, but the second one will be easier.

She was lucky, blessed, her mother said, that the baby was saved in time.

After his toast, James kisses Jeanne's cheek.

"Hear! Hear!" her brother says in his booming minister's voice.

Jeanne's eyes meet her husband's, and she wishes that a new spark would pass between them, something to connect them still, besides their child. She feels like crying, but she does not want to incite one of her mother's rants about her being a spoiled brat who needs to stop sulking and get on with her life. In all the time since her child was born and she realized that his birth would not necessarily make her joyful, and in all the time since she became aware that her mother's mind, as well as her mother's love, was slipping away, today at the church was the first time she has cried.

3

A week before Jude was born, Carole went to the Opa Locka Hialeah Flea Market, which Haitians call Ti Mache, and got some eucalyptus leaves and sour oranges for her daughter's first post-partum bath. She bought her daughter a corset and a few yards of white muslin, which she sewed into a bando for Jeanne to wrap around her belly. But because of the C-section, neither the bath nor the binding was possible, which was why her daughter's belly did not go back to the way it had been before. Jeanne became larger, in fact, because she refused to drink the fennel-and-aniseed infusions that both Carole and Grace brewed for her. And she refused to breastfeed, which not only would have melted her extra fat but would also have made her feel less sad.

When Jeanne and Paul were babies, no other woman was around to help. Carole didn't have the luxury of lying in bed while relatives took care of her and her children. Her husband did the best he could. He went out and got her the leaves and made her the teas. He gave her the baths himself. He helped her retie the bando every morning before he left for work, but during the hours that he was gone she was so lonely and homesick that she kept kissing her babies' faces, as if their cheeks were plots of land in the country she'd left behind.

She couldn't imagine life without her children.

She would have felt even more lost and purposeless without them. She wanted them both to have everything they desired. And whenever money was tight, especially after she and Victor bought their house in Miami's Little Haiti, she would clean other people's homes while her children were at school and her husband was at work, something her husband and children never knew about. Her secret income made him admire her even more. Every week, before he handed her the allowance for household expenses, he would proudly tell the children, "Your manman sure knows how to stretch a dollar."

Her cleaning money also paid for all the things her daughter believed she'd be a pariah without—brand-name sneakers and clothes, class rings, prom dresses. Her son wasn't interested in anything but books, and only library books at that. He would happily walk around with holes in his cheap shoes.

She should have told her daughter about the sacrifices she'd made. If she had, it would be easier now to tell her that she couldn't stay sad forever. Where would the family be if Carole had stayed sad when she arrived in this country? Sometimes you just have to shake the devil off you, whatever that devil is. Even if you don't feel like living for yourself, you have to start living for your child, for your children.

4

Jeanne doesn't realize that her husband and her mother have wandered off with Jude until she finds herself alone with her father.

She hasn't discussed her mother's condition with him for some time. She does not want to tell him or her husband how earlier in the week, when her mother was visiting, she'd forced herself to go out and sit by the pool while her son was napping. As soon as she put her feet in the water, she glanced up and saw her mother watching her from the terrace. Her mother looked bewildered, as though she had no idea where she was. Jeanne was in the middle of a phone call with James. She ended the call quickly and ran upstairs, and by the time she reached the apartment her mother was standing by the door. She pushed the door shut, grabbed Jeanne by the shoulders, and slammed her into it. Had Carole been bigger, she might have cracked open Jeanne's head.

Jeanne kept saying, "Manman, Manman," like an incantation, until it brought her back.

"What happened?" her mother asked.

Jeanne wanted to call an ambulance, or at least her father, but she was in shock, and her mother seemed fine the rest of the day. Jeanne avoided her as much as she could, let her watch a talk show she liked, and made sure that she was not left alone with Jude.

The next day, her mother showed up after James had gone to work and began shouting at her in Creole. "You have to fight the devil," she yelled. "Stop being selfish and living for yourself. Start living for your child."

Those incidents have made Jeanne afraid both of and for her mother. She agreed to go through with the christening in the hope that it might help. Perhaps her mother was only pretending to be losing her mind in order to get her way.

Sitting next to James on their living-room sofa, with Jude in her arms, Carole appears calmer than she has been all week. Paul is sitting on the other side of her, and the three of them seem to be talking about Jude, or about children in general. Then James's friend Marcos joins them, and Jude reaches out for his big cloud of an Afro.

Jeanne wonders how her brother could fail to notice that their mother is deteriorating. In all their conversations about the christening, he never mentioned Carole's state of mind. Was it because he was used to seeing her as a pious woman, not as his mother but as his "sister" in the Lord? Paul has never paid much attention to practical things. He spent most of their childhood reading books that even the adults they knew had never heard of, obscure novels and anthropological studies, the biographies of famous theologians and saints. Before he officially joined their mother's church, when he was a senior in high school, he had considered becoming a priest. He was always more concerned about the next world than he was about this one.

Her mother motions for Paul to scoot over, then lowers Jude into the space between them on the sofa. Jude turns his face back and forth and keeps looking up at the adults, especially at James.

"How are you these days?" Jeanne's father

asks. As he speaks to Jeanne, he's looking at her mother in a way she has never seen before, with neither admiration nor love but alarm, or even distress.

"Okay," she says. Usually that is enough for him. Her father, like her husband, doesn't normally push. But this time he does.

"Why do all this today?" her father asks, though he already knows the answer. "Did you have this child for her, too? Because she won't be able to take care of him for you. You'll have to do it for yourself."

"Of course I didn't have my son for her," Jeanne says.

"Then why have him?" he asks. "It doesn't seem like you want him."

This, whatever it is that she is feeling, she wants to tell him, isn't about not wanting her son. It's about not being up to the task; the job is too grand, too permanent, even with her husband's help. It's hard to explain to her father or to anyone else, but something that was supposed to kick in, maybe a light that was meant to turn on in her head, never did. Despite her complete physical transformation, at times she feels as though she has not given birth at all. It's not that she doesn't want her son, or wishes he hadn't been born; it's just that she can't believe that he is truly hers.

"What's really wrong with Manman?" she asks, desperate to change the subject.

"We're not done talking about you," her father says.

"What's wrong with her?" she insists.

"She's not herself," he says.

"It's more than that."

"What do you want me to say?"

"We need to know the truth."

"We," he says, pointing to her mother, then to himself, "already know the truth."

Jeanne hears her mother laughing, softly at first, then louder, at something that either James or Marcos has said. She realizes that possibly there have been doctors, a diagnosis, one that her parents are keeping to themselves.

"What are you saying?" she asks.

"I'll soon have to put her somewhere," he says.

She thinks of the expense and how her mother will not be the only one who is dislocated. Her father may have to sell the house in order to afford a decent place where her mother won't be neglected or abused. She thinks of the irony of her family's not being able to take care of her mother, who has dedicated so much of her life to them.

"I'm not saying it will happen tomorrow, but we'll have to put her somewhere one day."

Jeanne hasn't seen the pain in her father's face before, because she hasn't been looking for it. She hasn't been thinking about other people's pain at all. But now she can see the change in him. His hair is grayer and his voice drags. His eyes are red from lack of sleep, his face weathered with worry.

5

Carole and her childhood friend Jeanne used to talk to each other through a hole they'd poked in the plywood that separated their rooms. In the morning, when Jeanne went to fetch water at the neighborhood tap, she would whistle a wake-up call to Carole. Jeanne's whistle sounded like the squeaky chirping of a pipirit gri, the gray kingbirds that flew around the area until boys knocked them down with slingshots, roasted them in firepits, and ate them.

One morning, Jeanne did not whistle, and

Carole never saw her again. The boys in the neighborhood said that her mother had killed her and buried her, then disappeared, but Jeanne's mother had probably just been unable to make the rent and skipped out before daylight.

The next occupant of that room was Victor. Victor's father worked on a ship that traveled to Miami, and everyone in the neighborhood knew that Victor would be going there, too, one day. His father brought back suitcases full of clothes a couple of times a year, and Victor would always come over with some T-shirts or dresses that his mother said she had no use for. Victor soon discovered the hole in the plywood and would slip his finger through and wave it at Carole. Then she would whistle to him, like the last kingbird of their neighborhood.

Carole knew from the moment she met Victor that he would take care of her. She never thought he'd conspire against her, or even threaten to put her away. But here he is now, plotting against her with a woman she does not know, a fleshy, pretty woman, just the way he once liked them, just the way she was, when he liked her most.

Her husband and this woman are speaking in whispers. What are they talking about? And why is she sitting next to this peppercorn-haired doll that her husband sometimes uses to trick her, pretending it's a real baby. Her real babies are gone. They disappeared with her friend Jeanne, and all she has left is this doll her husband bought her.

She looks around the room to see if anyone realizes what's going on, how this young woman is stealing her husband from her right under her nose while she is stuck on this sofa between strangers and a propped-up baby doll. She grabs the doll by its armpits and raises it to her shoulder. The doll's facial expressions are so real, so lifelike, that its lips curl and its cheeks crumple as though it were actually about to cry. To calm it down, she whistles the pipirit's spirited squeak.

Carole is trying to explain all this to the men on either side of her, but they can't understand her. One of them holds his hands out to her as if he wants her to return the doll to him.

They are crowding around her now. The fleshy young woman, too, is moving closer. Carole doesn't understand what all the fuss is about. She just wants to take the doll out to the yard, the way she often does when her husband isn't around. She wants to feel the sun-filled breeze on her face and see the midday luster of the pool. She wants to prove to everyone that not only can she take care of herself but she can take care of this doll, too.

6

How does her mother get past James and Paul and run to the terrace with Jude in her arms? Jude is squirming and wailing, his bare pudgy legs cycling erratically as her mother dangles him over the terrace railing.

Her father is the first to reach the terrace, followed by James and everyone else. Though Carole is standing on the shady side of the terrace, she is sweating. Her bun has loosened as though Jude, or someone else, had been pulling at it.

Jeanne isn't sure how long her mother's bony arms will be able to support her son, especially since Jude is crying and twisting, all while turning his head toward the faces on the terrace as though he knows how desperate they are to have him back inside.

Paul has rushed downstairs, and Jeanne is

now looking down at her brother's face as she tries to figure out where her son might land if her mother drops him. The possibility of Jude landing in his uncle's arms is as slim or as great as Jude landing in the pool or on the ficus hedge below the terrace.

Marcos also appears down by the pool, as does James's sister, Zoe. James is on the phone with the Fire-Rescue. Jeanne's mother-in-law, Grace, has Jeanne caged in her arms, as if to keep Jeanne from crumbling to the floor. Jeanne's father is standing a few feet from her mother, begging, pleading.

Once James is off the phone, he switches places with Jeanne's father. Jude balls his small fists, reopens them, then aims both his hands at his father. He stops crying for a moment, as if waiting for James to grab him. When James reaches for him, Carole leans and pushes Jude farther out. Everyone gasps and, once Grace releases Jeanne, she doubles over, as if she had been sliced in two.

"Manman, please," Jeanne says, straightening herself up. "Souple Manman. Tanpri."

Other tenants come out of their apartments. Some are already on their terraces. Others are by the pool with Paul, Zoe, and Marcos. Her son at his last checkup weighed nineteen pounds, which is about a fifth of her mother's current weight. Her mother will not be able to hold on to him much longer.

Jeanne walks toward her husband, approaching carefully, brushing past her father, who appears to be in shock.

"Manman, please give me my baby," Jeanne says. She tries to speak in a firm and steady voice, one that will not frighten her son.

Her mother regards her with the dazed look that is now too familiar.

"Let me have him, Carole," Jeanne says. Maybe not being her daughter will give her more authority in her mother's eyes. Her mother may think that Jeanne is someone she has to listen to, someone she must obey.

"Baby," her mother says, and it sounds more like a term of endearment for Jeanne than the realization that she's holding a small child.

"Your baby?" Carole asks, her arms wavering now, as if she were finally feeling Jude's full weight.

Jeanne lowers her voice. "He's my child, Manman. Please give him to me."

Jeanne can see in the loosening of her mother's arms that she is returning. But her mother is still not fully back, and, if she returns too suddenly, she may get confused and drop Jude. While her mother's eyes are focused on her, Jeanne signals with a nod for her husband to move in, and, with one synchronized lurch, her father reaches for her mother, and her husband grabs their son. Her mother relaxes her grip on Jude only after he is safely back across the railing.

James collapses on the terrace floor, his still-crying son pressed tightly against his chest. Jeanne's father takes her mother by the hand and leads her back inside. He sits with her on the sofa and wraps his arms around her as she calmly rests her head on his shoulder.

Two police officers, two black women, arrive soon after. They are followed by EMTs. A light is shined in her mother's pupils by one of the EMTs, then her blood pressure is taken. Though her mother seems to have snapped out of her episode and now looks only tired, it's determined that Carole needs psychiatric evaluation. Jude is examined and has only some bruising under his armpits from his grandmother's tight grip.

Jeanne sees the dazed look return to her mother's eyes as she climbs onto the lowered gurney, with some help from Victor and from Paul. Her father asks that her mother not be strapped down, but the head EMT insists that it is procedure and promises not to hurt her.

Jeanne had hoped that her mother was only trying to teach her a lesson, to shock her out of her blues and remind her that she is capable of loving her son, but then she sees her mother's eyes as she is being strapped to the gurney. They are bleary and empty. She appears to be looking at Jeanne but is actually looking past her, at the wall, then at the ceiling.

Carole's body goes limp as the straps are snapped over her wrists and ankles, and it seems as though she were letting go completely, giving in to whatever has been ailing her. She seems to know that she'll never be back here, at least not in the way she was before. Jeanne knows, too, that this moment, unlike a birth, is no new beginning.

7

Carole wishes she'd see more of this, her daughter and her son-in-law together with their baby boy. James's arms are wrapped around his wife as she holds their son, who has fallen asleep.

Perhaps Jeanne will now realize how indispensable her son is to her. Carole regrets not telling her daughter a few of her stories. Now she will never get to tell them to her grandson, either. She will never play with him again.

The first time her husband took her to the doctor, before all the brain scans and spinal taps, the doctor asked about her family's medical history. He asked whether her parents or her grandparents had suffered from any mental illnesses, Alzheimer's, or dementia. She had not been able to answer any of his questions, because when he asked she could not remember anything about herself.

"She's not a good historian," the doctor told her husband, which was, according to Victor, the doctor's way of saying that she was incapable of telling her own life story.

She **is not** a good historian. She never has been. Even when she was well. Now she will never get a chance to be. Her grandson will grow up not knowing her. The single most memorable story that will exist about her and him will be of her dangling him off a terrace, in what some might see as an attempt to kill him. For her, all this will soon evaporate, fade away. But everyone else will remember.

They are about to roll her out of the apartment on the gurney. Although her wrists are strapped down, her son is holding her left hand tightly. Jeanne gives Jude to his other grandmother and walks over to the gurney. She moves her face so close to Carole's that Carole thinks she is going to bite her. But then Jeanne pulls back, and it occurs to Carole that she is playing Alo, Bye, another peekaboo game her children used to enjoy. With their faces nearly touching, Jeanne crinkles her nose and whispers, "Alo, Manman," then "Bye, Manman."

It would be appropriate, if only she could make herself believe that this is what her daughter is actually doing. It would be a fitting close to her family life, or at least to life with her children. You are always saying hello to them while preparing them to say goodbye to you. You are always dreading the separations, while cheering them on, to get bigger, smarter, to crawl, babble, walk, speak, to have birthdays that you hope you'll live to see, that you pray they'll live to see. Jeanne will now know what it's like to live that way, to have a part of yourself walking around unattached to you, and to love that part so much that you sometimes feel as though you were losing your mind.

Her daughter reaches down and takes her right hand, so that both of her children are now holding her scrawny, shaky hands, which seem not to belong to her at all.

"Mèsi, Manman," her daughter says. "Thank you."

There is nothing to thank her for. She has only done her job, her duty as a parent. There is no longer any need for hellos or goodbyes, either. Soon there will be nothing left, no past to cling to, no future to hope for. Only now.

Seven Stories

As the plane was landing, I pressed my forehead against the window to check out the island from my seat. The airport was surrounded by a barbed-wire-topped concrete wall that was interrupted in some places by patches of bougainvillea and bamboo palms, which seemed to have been strategically placed to hide still-visible cracks. Everything outside the perimeter was dangerous. Or so the main windowless, bunkerlike terminal seemed to indicate. I might be better off taking the next plane back, I thought. But I'd been personally invited by the island's prime minister's wife.

"My dearest Kim," Callie Morrissete had written me a few weeks back from her private e-mail account. "I read your essay about that life-changing month (at least for me) we spent together in Brooklyn when we were little girls.

I've been waiting so long to see you again and will have more free time than usual over the holidays. I will make all the arrangements. Please come!"

It was late afternoon on New Year's Eve and a roasting ninety degrees, even in the Caribbean shade. The other passengers in the terminal were mainly tourists or locals returning home from colder climates. The returning locals were dragging oversize hand luggage bursting with gifts for their loved ones. The rest of the passengers were white missionaries, mostly older men, but some women and college students of both sexes, too. On the front of their T-shirts was the phrase TOUCH LIVES NOW, SAVE SOULS FOREVER. The dates of their weeklong revival, which were printed on the back of their T-shirts, happened to coincide with my stay, from New Year's Eve to the day after Three Kings' Day. I'd thought about staying longer, but I didn't want to abuse my hostess's hospitality. After all, we hadn't seen each other since we were seven years old.

A young bearded protocol officer met me as I entered the main building. He was holding an enlarged version of my author photo from the online magazine where I was a staff writer. I was wearing tons of makeup in the picture, and now, blown up on an eight-by-twelve foam poster board, my oval face, wide nose, too-close-together eyes, and curly half bun looked like they all belonged on a clown.

The protocol officer signaled for me to follow him to a luxurious lounge, whose bright marble floors were covered with Persian rugs, bordered by alligator-skin sofas. On the front-room walls, surrounding the official portraits of Callie and her husband, Gregory Murray, were nearly a dozen watercolors of considerable size and with extensive floral details.

In the last year or so, I had occasionally looked Callie up online and recently found some articles describing her pet initiatives, from vaccination campaigns to disaster preparedness for the quarter of a million or so people on their island of about a thousand square miles. In her first newspaper interview as the prime minister's wife, she promised that she'd push her husband to "do his best," that she wouldn't hesitate to criticize him publicly if she saw him slacking.

"I married my wife not just for her beauty but also for her strong mind," her husband was quoted as saying in the same article. "She is a citizen of this country with the same rights as every other citizen to speak as freely as she wishes."

Callie's father, Charles Morrissete, the island's most famous prime minister, was assassinated by one of his security guards when Callie was seven years old. Her mother fled with her to Prospect Park South in Brooklyn, seeking refuge with Miss Ruby, our next-door neighbor, who was Callie's mother's aunt. A few weeks later, after the assassin was caught, tried, and jailed, and was himself assassinated in prison, Callie and her mother returned to the island, taking Miss Ruby with them. Over the years, there were several failed election attempts while the country was being run by a council of citizen advisers, a kind of board of directors. Finally, two decades later, Callie's husband, who was a child of the island's oligarchy and had been working as one of the government council's youngest lawyers, was elected by the majority of eligible voters, who, like their new prime minister, were under thirty years old.

Callie Morrissete walked into the airport lounge wearing a short, body-hugging bottle-green dress that was belted around her tiny waist. Her only jewelry was some gold hoop earrings and a thin platinum wedding band on her long tapering fingers. She looked like a runway model on her day off, flaunting her flawless onyx skin and her short dark hair, blown out and tucked behind her ears. Callie and I were about the same height when we were seven; she now towered over me in high-heeled strappy red sandals.

"It's good to see you, Kim." She spoke with a trained accent that merged French, English, Spanish, and Dutch, all languages she'd grown up speaking on the island. At seven, she had been mostly an English speaker, her voice not that different from mine. Or at least that's what I'd thought.

Her husband was standing behind her, waiting his turn to say hello. He was with an entourage of half a dozen dark-suit-clad men and women, whom I suspected were part of his security detail. He, too, looked a lot like he did in his pictures, including the official one on the wall. An imposing tall and muscular man, he had a square, ocher, sharply defined face. Looking at them standing side by side, him in a tan suit that I was sure Callie had picked out for him, I couldn't help but wonder what he was doing when **he** was seven years old.

Seven

By Kimberly Boyer

. . . When she first came to Brooklyn, my scrawny and sad friend cried herself to sleep every night. Her father, her country's prime minister, had been driven outside the city limits by one of his bodyguards and shot. Her mother's elderly aunt, Miss Ruby, who lived next door to us in a large Victorian house filled with elaborate embroideries and rococo furniture from their island nation, was the one who brought us together.

The first time this friend came to my house she was crying. My parents—pediatricians both—brought her to my room and, with pleading looks in their eyes, asked me to entertain her as she sobbed.

When my mom and dad shut the door behind them, I walked over to where she was leaning against the wall, bawling in her hands, and asked her what game she wanted to play. I expected her to bark at me and run for the door, but she didn't. She just stood there and continued to cry.

I didn't know much about her situation. My mother had simply told me that a little girl who was special to Miss Ruby was coming over and that she had "suffered a great loss."

"What's your great loss?" I'd asked my new friend.

She was taken off guard. Perhaps this was not the question she was expecting as a follow-up to "What do you want to play?" She raised her face from her hands and stopped crying long enough to say, "Everybody is going to die."

"That's not true," I said, because if everybody was going to die, my parents and I would also be dying and I did not want us to die.

"Everybody in my country is going to die," she clarified.

I considered this for a moment, then asked, "You have a country?"

"Yes, I have a country," she answered, her pride at knowing more about the world than me momentarily comforting her.

"This is not your country?" I asked.

"Here? No!"

"Tell me about your country then," I said.

"My country is green," she said. "And warm."

Her country, in other words, was everything Brooklyn was not in the winter.

"We have beaches," she continued. "Lots of them. The beaches have different-color sand. White. Black. Gray. Pink. Gold. My father once showed me a golden beach at sunrise."

She looked up at my stenciled ceiling as though she was trying to imagine a more idyllic world. I knew my parents were probably listening outside the door, and when she started crying again, my mother reappeared.

My mother's presence made her stop, and when my mother left the room this time, my friend did not cry. After hearing about her country, I realized that I had never heard of it. It was possible that everybody there was going to die.

"I'm sorry about your country," I said, then I asked her again, "What do you want to play?"

She looked at me the way my parents did sometimes, when they told me something I was supposed to understand but didn't.

"Why do you think everybody's going to die?" I sat on the edge of my bed and motioned for her to come sit next to me.

"Because my father is dead," she said, not budging.

"Are you sure?"

"My mum keeps saying it, so it must be true."

She looked like she was going to start crying again, so I lay on the bed, my arms stiffened at my side, as my grandmother's had been in her coffin the year before when she died. I closed my eyes and said, "Now I'm dead, too."

"You can't be dead if you're talking," she said.

I fell silent for a while. My friend began singing what she called a funeral hymn, which I would later realize was "Ave Maria."

We spent the rest of the afternoon playing funeral, taking turns at being the cadaver and the priest. My mother interrupted us with some fruit snacks, but as soon as she was gone we started playing funeral again.

My parents rarely attended church, except for weddings and funerals, like my grandmother's. But since it was part of my friend's family's job to attend Mass on official occasions in her country, she knew many songs to sing for the dead.

My friend returned to my house every afternoon when I was done with my homework. After spending the day being homeschooled by Miss Ruby, she was ready to play. She got tired of funeral and became interested in other games. I was so happy that, with my mother's approval, I gave her a box of hair ribbons I'd had since I was little. We baked imaginary cakes in my Easy-Bake Oven, had tea parties with my stuffed animals and dolls, and played dress-up with my princess gowns, which were nowhere near as ruffled, flowered, and embroidered as the actual ankle-length dresses Miss Ruby bought her. When she changed out of those dresses and into my princess gowns, she went into the closet and closed the door, and because she was used to giving orders, I listened when she told me that I was not to disturb her there.

Every now and then, my mother would let us watch thirty minutes of cartoons in our princess dresses. My friend's favorite moment, though, was when we played Seven Stories, a game she used to play with her father. We would list an important moment from each of the seven years we had been alive.

"My first year, I was born," she would say. "My second year, I walked and talked. My third year, I fell and scraped my knee when I ran away from my governess." She raised her dress to show me the crescent-shaped scar on her right knee, which I hadn't noticed before. "My fourth year, I started early school."

"You mean preschool," I interrupted her. I was glad to have a chance to correct her.

"We call some things by different names in my country." She grimaced, seeming annoyed at being interrupted.

"My fourth year, I started preschool," she continued. "My fifth year, Daddy became prime minister," she went on, ignoring me altogether. "My sixth year, I moved into a castle. My seventh year, Daddy died."

Until then I had not given much thought to my seven years of life. My first year, I'd learned from my mother, I stopped nursing. My second year, my parents moved into the house we were now living in. My third year, my mother's mother, Grandma Rose, came to live with us. My fourth year, I started preschool and got sick so often that my mother pulled me out and Grandma Rose taught me how to read. My fifth year, I started regular school again when Grandma Rose got cancer in her belly. My sixth year, Grandma Rose died. My seventh year, Callie Morrissete arrived, crying into my life . . .

In the armored SUV in the middle of the mile-long motorcade taking us to the prime minister's residence in the hills, I didn't ask about the landslide election that had brought the island's first millennial prime minister to power. Instead I asked Callie how she and her husband met.

As Callie described how they'd been part of the same social circles since they were born, and how the only reason they didn't attend the same schools was because her mother had always put her in girls' schools with nuns, and how they'd still attended the same parties as teenagers and even later when they were home on vacation from their different University of the West Indies campuses, Callie's husband—who told me to call him Greg—reached over and placed his hand on her lap, then interrupted her to explain that he'd purposely been putting himself in her path since they were born.

"There's never been anyone else for me," Greg said.

Back in the 1950s, when the island was a tax shelter and one of many tropical playgrounds for the world's rich and famous, the sprawling five-story residence, where the island's most recent leaders, including Callie's family, lived, had been a five-star hotel. Built on ten secluded acres, it had its own outdoor nightclub and rooftop garden.

As the motorcade pulled into the property's winding driveway, the centerpiece of which was a colossal wedding-cake-shaped water fountain, the car ahead of us abruptly stopped, and the security people jumped out.

"Home, sweet home," Callie said, trying perhaps to put me at ease.

I felt as though I knew the place somewhat, both from the pictures I'd seen of it online and the way Callie had described it during our afternoon playdates. She had called it a castle and told me that it was one of the biggest buildings on the island, a fortress filled with great hiding places. It was a wonderful place to live, she'd said, except that grown-ups with guns were always watching over her.

Once we were out of the car, Greg excused himself and walked to the east wing of the property, followed by his entourage.

"Would you like to see where you're staying?" Callie asked.

We were left with two female security guards, whom Callie waved away, but rather than leave her alone completely, they took a few steps back as we walked into the residence's high-vaulted lobby and into a glass elevator.

As the elevator rose, I could see the water fountain and the winding driveway and the top of Greg's head, along with his entourage of security people. Based on the articles I'd read both in international publications and in the island's own newspapers, it seemed as though he and Callie were very popular. Promising to be a reformer, Greg had become prime minister under the banner of her father's MRP, or Major Reform Party, which was perhaps never more revered on the island than when Callie's father was at the helm.

We got off the elevator on the top floor, and before she could open the door, one of Callie's female security guards walked out of a service elevator with my suitcase, opened the door for us, and followed us inside.

The guest suite was nearly the size of my parents' house to which I'd returned after graduating from college six years before, in part to save money until I could earn more. This is not something I was proud of. Not that I expected to be the prime minister of a Caribbean island

nation, or the spouse of one, but I thought I'd
be much further along in my career than I was.

The terrace in the guest suite at the prime
minister's residence had a panoramic view of
the capital city. On the outer limits of the city
was the seaport. In the harbor was a cruise
ship, which was the other way Callie had suggested for me to come. Not far from the seaport was the airport. Then the old city, where,
Callie pointed out, Taino, Arawak, and Carib
villages had been re-created, with replicas of
round thatched-roof homes. In the old city
were baroque- and Gothic-style forts from the
colonial period when the island was ruled by
Europeans of different stripes. Some of the old
châteaus bordering once-thriving sugar, cotton,
coffee, and tobacco plantations were in ruins,
which tourists visited every day. In the newer
parts of the city were the government offices,
courts, hospitals, high-rises and fancy hotels,
markets—both open and covered—and a ba-
silica. On many of the hills surrounding the
downtown area, tin shacks and finished and un-
finished concrete houses were crammed next to
one another. Their outer walls were painted in
bright pinks, yellows, and greens, as if some effort had been made to turn them into a splashy

collage meant to be admired from afar. On top of those hills were mansions, villas, palacios surrounded by glass-shard-capped walls.

"So this is your country?" I said, remembering how she'd seemed insulted that I didn't instantly realize when we met that she was from somewhere else.

"Part of it," she said.

We walked back into the suite, which had a fireplace, bordered with frescoes depicting moments from the island's history, including a scene at a slave port showing whip-wielding European traders next to a line of naked broad-chested African teenage boys and wide-hipped young women.

"I believe he's ready for you, madame," the female security guard who'd carried my suitcase inside said.

"I've arranged a treat for us," Callie said.

I followed her down a long hallway whose walls and ceiling were covered in gold leaf. Another suite similar to the one I was staying in was being used as Callie's dressing room.

"I hope you don't mind," Callie said after we walked in. "I had my stylist bring some dresses for you. In different sizes, because I wasn't sure."

A young man pushed a clothes rack forward

and parked it between her and me. He began pulling out sequined and beaded evening gowns and holding them up against my body. I remembered playing dress-up with Callie during the time we spent together in Brooklyn. As we sipped pretend tea in my room, in my princess gowns, it was obvious even then that only one of us was **playing** at being a princess. Now it seemed as though we were playing dress-up again. I tried on gown after gown while she gave a thumbs-up or -down. I eventually settled on a formal yet comfortable black mermaid gown.

"At the end of your essay 'Seven,'" Callie said while I was twirling around in the mermaid gown, "you wrote that after we left New York, you stopped believing in princesses, castles, and fairy tales. Is that true?"

I stopped twirling. I had hoped that she might read my essay, but I didn't think it would lead to my being invited to the island to provide further clarification.

"I'm not unhappy you didn't use my name," she said as I struggled to come up with an answer. "I'm glad you didn't name the island. Only people who know can figure it out. But I'll tell you right now, there was no fairy tale.

My mother thought a lot of people wanted me and her dead as well."

I was starting to wonder whether she was upset about the essay, which was different from any writing I'd done for the online magazine. I mostly wrote reviews of live and recorded music, streamed and cable shows, movies, and some visual art. I had stepped out of my comfort zone to write that essay, which was part of a popular series on childhood.

"Tell me, Cal, does your stylist have a few guys, too, in different sizes, lying around?" I asked, trying to change the subject.

"We have a couple of ministers who are not old geezers," she said. "The last of the single ones, though, is engaged to be married."

"What's the engaged one minister of?" I asked.

"Finance," she said.

After we ate—a huge, delicious chicken-and-mango salad—showered, and got our hair and makeup done by someone on her staff, Callie went downstairs to find her husband. I went back to the guest suite and googled Finance. Finance was one of Greg's closest friends. He was short and brawny, like a bodybuilder. He was also one of the island's most eligible bachelors, a national playboy. His last two semiserious girlfriends, before he got engaged, had been a singer from Barbados and an actress from Aruba. In all of his pictures, every coiled-hair strand was in place. He looked like he spent a lot of time in front of the mirror.

The prime minister's New Year's Eve gala was held under a tent near the outdoor nightclub behind the residence. Callie and Greg were both dressed in white, him in an embroidered dashiki pant set, and her in an off-the-shoulder, toga-inspired gown, which in the intentionally golden lighting inside the tent made them both glow. As they welcomed the guests in the receiving line, Greg seemed to follow Callie's lead, offering the same level of delight or coldness she did. She, then in turn he, would embrace some of the pairs warmly—they were mostly couples—then would barely wave to others.

I watched all this from a few feet away, at the head table, which was smaller than the other hundred or so tables, which were all decorated with white candles and tall bouquets of white hibiscus. Scattered on the tables were also party hats, horns, and flutes. I was sitting next to the one other guest at the head table so far, Callie's mother. She was wearing a black pantsuit, a pink conch-pearl choker with matching studs, and a large vintage filigree butterfly brooch.

During their time in New York, I'd rarely seen Callie's mother. She had mostly stayed inside Miss Ruby's house. Whenever Callie came over to play, Miss Ruby was the one who brought her. I only heard Mrs. Morrissete speak briefly on their last night in Brooklyn, when Miss Ruby invited us over for a farewell dinner.

At that dinner, Mrs. Morrissete said—in a hoarse voice, with a puffy face and red eyes that matched Callie's—that she was returning to the island because that's all she had left besides Callie. That night, as Callie ignored her dinner and sat watching teary eyed, I'd also learned, based on the questions my parents had gently asked Miss Ruby, that the Africans who'd been brought to the island by Europeans as slaves centuries before were mostly Ibo, Nago, Fula, and Dahomey. (I had listened closely so I could picture what my weepy friend was returning to.) I also learned that the unexplored land beneath the island was full of copper, silver, and gold. While Miss Ruby was talking, about midway into the meal, Mrs. Morrissete excused herself and retired to her room. Callie quickly followed.

Mrs. Morrissete seemed no happier now than she had been in Brooklyn. Her slumped shoulders, quivering jaw, and alternating vacant stare and downcast eyes remained the same as they had been at dinner that night. I offered her my condolences about Miss Ruby, who, I'd learned in my e-mail exchanges with Callie, died a few years after they returned to the island. Callie had also shared in those e-mails that Mrs. Morrissete was living in the same suite in the prime minister's residence that the three of them had occupied as a family, and that she rarely ventured out in public anymore, except once or twice a year.

Finance arrived in a tuxedo with his fiancée, a four-time Olympian gold-medalist runner who was still considered one of the world's fastest women. She was wearing a fitted silver gown and was so beloved that she got a standing ovation as she and Finance walked to their seats at the head table. Perhaps to not upset Callie and Greg, everyone remained standing until he and Callie also sat down.

After the table filled up with Greg's parents and a few older couples who were obviously important government officials or simply well-connected folks, Callie and Greg, Finance and the Runner, and I left Mrs. Morrissete and the elders to their muted conversations and formed a kind of youthful clique, discussing everything from the latest worldwide music and dance crazes, to gossiping about sports celebrities the Runner knew, to discussing issue-oriented documentaries and podcasts, and rating popular movies and shows we'd binge-watched, me for work, them for fun.

Every once in a while Greg and Finance would allow the rest of the table in and, once they'd gotten past the personal banter, lead their elders to issues they felt had been neglected in the past, like gender-based violence, gender equality, same-sex marriage, and marijuana legalization, which Finance thought could bring in much-needed revenue. One of the older men at the table abruptly told Greg that he would be better off trying to come up with a decent immigration plan.

"Most immigration plans are essentially anti-immigration plans," Callie, who had studied international affairs at university, said, defending her husband.

"With all due respect, my dear lady," the old

man said, "we have to do something about all the Haitians who keep washing up on our shores."

"My friend Kimberly here is Haitian," Callie said, cutting him off. "Her parents are from Haiti."

The table grew quiet. Everyone turned to look at me, as if to search in my face and demeanor for traces of whatever types of Haitians they were most familiar with.

"Human beings have been migrating since the beginning of time," I said, trying to sound as coolly authoritative as the old man, while picking up one of the New Year's Eve party horns, which I wanted to blow in the old man's face.

"It's of course not uncommon for people to look for better opportunities elsewhere," I continued. "I bet some of your own people travel . . . when they want or need more than what they can get here."

"Forgive me for being crass," the old man interrupted me. "But we need people who offer more as well. Not just those who take from us." Then turning to Greg, the old man added in a tone that was meant to conclude the discussion, "If your wife's emotions become the arbiters of your policy, then you won't last very long in your current position."

I put the party horn down and tried even

harder not to feel angry. After all, there were people like this everywhere who felt the same way about some group or other. But New Year's Day is also Haitian Independence Day, so the old man might have focused on that instead.

"Don't worry. I'm not planning to stay," I said, doing my best to lighten things up a bit.

Greg gave the old man a scolding glare, then motioned to someone on his staff to walk over to the bass player fronting the live band in a poorly lit side corner of the tent. The live band and a DJ were taking turns playing the party's background music, and Greg now wanted the band to play.

Callie and Greg got up to dance. My table-mates followed. The only people not dancing were me and Mrs. Morrissete, whose down-turned mouth flowered into a delicate smile as she watched her daughter waltz across the dance floor with her tall and elegant husband.

After their waltz, Callie, Finance, and the Runner sat down, and I ended up with Greg's well-manicured hand extended toward me.

"Don't worry. I wouldn't make you waltz," he said.

The DJ began playing a slow American ballad, one of those whose ubiquity we'd been criticizing earlier. I laughed at the coincidence. Or maybe it wasn't a coincidence at all.

"I'm so glad you accepted Cal's invitation," he said. His accent, like Callie's, blended many languages, but he sounded much more like everyone else on the island whom I'd heard speak so far.

"I'm glad she invited me," I said.

"Cal's been talking about you for years," he said. "Even though you were together for such a short time, it marked her greatly."

I, too, had thought about Callie now and then, wondering how she'd fared after returning to her homeland. Right after Callie's mother took Callie and Miss Ruby back to the island, my parents would call Miss Ruby once in a while, but after a few months either Miss Ruby's number changed or she stopped responding. I once heard my parents say that they hoped Callie was getting the proper help and that her mother and great-aunt would not continue to act as though nothing life changing had happened to her.

When I was in high school, my parents found a few pictures my dad had taken of me and Callie playing. They mentioned going on vacation to the island, but they never did more than talk about it. Callie crossed my mind again in college, but she was impossible to track. She had no digital footprint until her husband became prime minister.

"I'm sorry about my countryman's xenophobia," Greg said while wrapping one hand around my waist and pinning the other to my shoulder blade. He looped me in a semicircle, then rotated back. I tried to let myself relax. He was a good dancer, the kind that does all the work.

"Please just tell me that the guy who wants all my people out is not in charge of immigration," I said. Our damp cheeks had to touch so he could hear me over the music.

"He's not," he said. "He's a friend of my parents."

I was about to ask if the Runner was also a family friend when he said, "I read your essay."

"You did?"

"Cal showed it to me."

"What did you think?" Should I feel anxious about the piece, I wondered. My recollection of an old childhood memory seemed to mean even more to these people than I ever imagined.

"I was still young when it happened," he said, "but there were some terrible rumors within our very small circle about how Cal and her mum got off the island the day her father was killed."

I glanced over at the table, at the seat where Mrs. Morrissete had been sitting. It was empty. I looked around the tent trying to spot her, but I didn't see her anywhere.

"What kind of rumors?" I asked. I didn't want to pry, but it seemed as though he wanted me to ask.

"Cal's father was betrayed even though he was a great prime minister." He pulled me slightly closer, as though he did not want me to miss a word. "He lowered unemployment, increased tourism. He built more roads, schools, and hospitals than anyone had before him. Our goal is to follow in his footsteps."

"Was there more to his death than just the security guard?" I asked.

"There were some rumors to that as well," he said, "but only the guard was punished."

I looked over at the table where Callie was chatting with Finance and the Runner. I found the song her husband and I were dancing to rather long, then I realized that it had changed to another nearly identical ballad without my noticing.

When the ballad ended, I heard the A section

of a jazz tune, the sound of bass strings being plucked. We stopped dancing, as did everyone else on the dance floor, and turned our attention to the live band. The bass grew louder, then a snappy saxophone and sprightly trombone joined in. The bass hook returned as a bridge to the keyboard and drums until all the instruments sounded like a chorus of primal screams.

"I requested that for you," Greg leaned forward and whispered when the piece ended. "Charles Mingus's 'Haitian Fight Song.' It's my apology to you on behalf of my family friend."

Before I could say anything, the master of ceremonies, a local TV personality, announced that it was almost midnight. Servers appeared with Champagne bottles and flutes as ushers, dressed in the black and gold of the country's flag, guided everyone outside to watch the fireworks. Greg quickly walked away. Other party guests kept stopping him as he tried to make his way back to Callie. I soon lost track of them both as everyone spilled out onto the lawn.

At midnight came the sounds of horns blaring and corks popping and Champagne glasses clinking and the fireworks exploding in the sky while everyone shouted "Happy New Year." I spotted Finance and the Runner and Callie and Greg up front, taking turns embracing one another. I wandered around the grounds until I found a quiet corner to call my parents to wish them a Happy New Year. No matter where I was, they always liked me to be the first person to speak to them on New Year's.

"Is Callie okay?" they kept asking after we'd quickly wished each other the best for the year ahead, and a happy Haitian Independence Day.

"She seems fine," I said.

"And her mother?" my father asked.

"She seems fine, too," I said, though I wasn't sure.

"Oh good," my mother said, sounding relieved.

Somehow Callie appeared by my side after I hung up with my parents.

"I've been looking for you," she said. "I want to show you something."

The residence's rooftop garden was bordered with concrete planters filled with red bromeliads, angel's-trumpets, and birds-of-paradise. The lingering smoke from the fireworks filled the air, intermingling with the more pleasant scent of the flowers. At every turn was some telltale sign of Callie's taste, which I now recognized from all my reading about her new life since I had accepted her invitation. Maquettes and kinetic sculptures followed by rows of rare orchids. A hand-carved bar with hammocks and cabanas, and under a light-strung canopy a long rosewood dining table positioned for the most far-reaching views of the city.

Two men in tuxedos were following us. They tried to be discreet, but their constant whispering into their cuff links gave them away. They even followed us to the waist-high glass railing, which made it appear as though there were no barriers between us and the view.

I was going to ask Callie about her mother when she said, "I want you to see this."

She pointed to some coils of light winding their way throughout the city. They were people, hundreds of them, dressed in white and carrying candles as they walked toward the port and the sea.

"It's called a shedding," she said. "As you walk to the sea, you shed from both your body and spirit all the awful things that have happened to you in the previous year."

"Have you ever done it?" I asked.

"Every year, after I came back here, with Aunt Ruby and my mum," she said. "And with

Greg, too, when I was older. He proposed to me at the beach after a procession like this three years ago."

"Madame," one of the security men said. "The PM's ready to begin his address."

The live broadcast of the prime minister's address was in the residence's main sitting room, whose most notable features were its high cathedral ceiling and the sheer-white, all-around, floor-to-ceiling curtains. When she arrived, Callie gently stroked her husband's cheeks as he was getting powder dabbed on his face.

"I thought you'd skipped out on me," he said.

"Sir, we're ready," the young cameraman said.

Callie stepped aside right before Greg began speaking.

"Brothers and sisters," he said to the camera. "Our ancestors were forced to abandon everything they knew. Some jumped off slave ships because they were seduced by the dream of an eternal freedom. Our ancestors must have surely dreamed of a day like this when we would gather to freely enjoy the bounties of our own land for yet another year. We start this New Year grateful for both our triumphs and our pain. We start this New Year anticipating the future we are creating for generations to come. My wife, Callie, and I wish you and your families a healthy, prosperous, and joyous New Year."

I imagined people watching him and being full of hope. It wasn't so much what he'd said, but how he said it. Perhaps it was the tone of his voice—calm, measured, confident—like a father making unbreakable promises to his children.

I did not see them enter the room, but before Callie and I could, Finance and the Runner walked over to congratulate their friend on his address. Callie drifted over, and I could see in their lighthearted four-way razzing and easy laughter a kind of luminosity.

"I'm going to bed." Greg reached for Callie, drawing her onto his lap as she wrapped her arms around his neck. "Cal and I have the children's hospital visit tomorrow."

"Settle this old people's early-to-bed business between the two of you, then," Finance said while playfully jabbing at his friend's biceps. "We're getting out of here before this thing catches."

I only got a few hours of sleep before it was time to go on the children's hospital visit. For some reason, I thought Callie and Greg would show up somewhere unexpectedly and surprise some neglectful staff, who would then be shamed and punished for their misdeeds. Or maybe that's what I was hoping would happen. Instead they were led, with cameras rolling, to spotless wards filled with children clad in new hospital-issued pajamas. The children barely looked sick as they lay in their pristine beds, some with snow-white casts on their legs and full IVs attached to their arms. Callie and Greg took pictures with the staff, pinched the cheeks and stroked the heads of the children. This seemed to be Greg's favorite part, as he lingered by the beds and tickled the feet of and made faces at the kids, who'd obviously been told to be on their best behavior and maybe even to smile.

In the car on the way back to the residence, sitting with his wife between us, Greg asked me what I thought of the visit.

"Interesting," I said, lying.

But he could see that I was lying and mock gasped. "Oh no! You caught on that they staged all of that. There's no way around it. Unless we just show up without letting them know, and doing that might mean embarrassing them on New Year's Day."

"Frankly, there's no way you can see the real country with us," Callie said. "I'm going to ask one of the security guys to take you around tomorrow. He'll take you wherever you want to go."

I would still be a voyeur, but at least I'd be out of their bubble for a few hours.

"When your father was PM, did he hate the stagecraft of these things as much as we do?" Greg asked Callie.

"He quite enjoyed it," she said. Then turning to face me, she said, "I was with Daddy on the morning of the day he died. His last visit was to an orphanage for blind children. He dropped me off at school afterward, went to work, and never came home."

Greg reached over and wrapped his arms around her when it seemed like she was fighting back tears. We sat there and listened to the hum and vibration of the speeding car for a while.

"I was in school, too, when it happened," Greg said, filling in our silence. "My mother came and got me, just like a lot of the other parents picked up their children that day. My parents were working for the Health Ministry then. We got in the car and drove to the airport. We got on a plane, a charter arranged by a few families. We spent the same amount of time Callie spent away, except we were in Belize, waiting it out."

I wondered why Callie and her mother did not go on the chartered plane with them.

"In any case, let's change the subject," Greg said. "Kim, tell me more about what she was like in New York with you when she was a little girl."

"She was unbearable," I joked.

"Not true!" Callie protested.

I thought of one of the moments I couldn't fit into the essay, about the first time Callie saw snow.

We had woken up, I told Greg, to find our street blanketed in white. My mother asked Miss Ruby if Callie would come out with us to Prospect Park. Callie, bouncing from foot to foot, squealed with delight as she attacked whole fields of untouched snow with the winter boots I lent her, leaving a line of sunken tracks everywhere we went. I was so thrilled to be showing her something she had never seen before. Still, she refused to stick her tongue out and catch some of the snow like I did.

"What if it kept falling but inside of me?" she asked.

Greg pushed his head back and laughed.

"I can't wait to share these stories with our children," he said.

What I did not tell him was that on the way home from Prospect Park that day, Callie had asked my mother if she could stay with us in New York and not return to the island. My mother and I each held one of her gloved hands as my mother knelt down and assured her that her mother loved her and would always keep her safe. That's probably all my mother thought she could say.

I suspected even then that there were many conversations between my mother and Miss Ruby, and maybe even with Mrs. Morrissete, about Callie not returning to the island too soon. But it was decided a month after her father had died, after his killer was captured and jailed, that it was okay for everyone to go back.

Callie found me as inconspicuous a tour guide as possible, a man in his sixties, who never stopped chewing gum, and who wore jeans and a white T-shirt and a backward baseball cap. On the way to town, he asked me to sit in the front passenger seat of what seemed like his own off-road vehicle so that he could more easily point out the sites he didn't want me to miss.

There was the waterfront fish market, with dozens of men and women sitting under umbrellas while selling seafood so fresh the fish were still writhing in coolers and baskets. Then the Carnival Museum, whose entrance was decorated with a mural featuring a female reveler in a sequined thong and feathered headdress. Then the Botanical Garden, which was said to have one of the oldest breadfruit trees in the world. Then the casino, which rivaled any casino in Las Vegas with its blinding glass façade and its equally opulent adjoining hotel. Then the courthouse and the National Penitentiary, both bright yellow buildings whose outside walls were even higher than the adjacent fort, which had been used as a dungeon and torture chamber during colonial days.

The driver was giving me a cursory view, a taste, of everything, he said, and later if I wanted to come back and look more closely, I should tell him.

"Can you show me a real hospital?" I asked.

The request sounded insulting, even to me. Still, the driver seemed to understand what I meant. Before I could elaborate further, he left the main road and found a side trail that narrowed into a hilly dirt path littered with flattened foam containers, plastic water bottles, and old clothes and rags half-buried in the red soil. On one side of the car was a line of men washing their motos for hire in a muddy stream, and on the other side women were cooking food for sale in large pots resting on boulders and sticks. This was probably one of the shantytowns I'd seen from the residence terrace.

The driver rolled down the window, perhaps so I could smell the charcoal turning to ash under the cooking pots and the fumes coming from the motos zooming by. I heard some of the island's patois being spoken between the food vendors and their customers as they haggled.

"Since that what you lookin' to see, yes, nou have poor peoples, too," the driver said, dragging his words as if to taunt me.

The road narrowed farther, and we passed lean-tos covered with corrugated tin, some with frayed sheets hanging on clotheslines out front. There were children everywhere. Minors apparently made up nearly a quarter of the island's population. The children were on rooftops—where there were rooftops—flying kites. They were gathered in circles on the ground—where the ground was not muddy—playing marbles. They appeared suddenly in the middle of the road, young girls and boys hovering near the food vendors.

The hospital occupied an entire block on a street that was also filled with dozens of small pharmacies. At the gate, which was being minded by armed guards, were medicine hawkers, who shoved a list of their products in front of whoever was entering or leaving the grounds.

The hospital's front lawn was crammed with people lying on bedsheets or pieces of cardboard. Those on the ground had been triaged, while those standing on the long line leading to the back of the box-shaped two-story building were still waiting to be given numbers.

Under a blooming ylang-ylang tree was the mothers' and children's corner. Many of the pregnant women there were with female relatives or partners, who occasionally offered them water or fanned away flies. The parents of sick children sweated and fidgeted. Some mouthed prayers while cradling miniature versions of themselves.

Among the children with chest-racking coughs and wounds wrapped in blood-soaked blouses or shirts, I spotted a little girl whose emaciated frame could be seen through her spotless white Communion dress. Her thinning hair was swept up in a tight Afro puff in the middle of her head. Her eyes fluttered as though she was too tired to stay awake. She looked like she might be the same age Callie and I were when we met.

I thought of my pediatrician parents who had been taking care of sick children all my life, children less sick than the ones I was looking at. I understood why, as doctors and potential healers, they'd wanted me to follow in their footsteps. I also knew why I could never do that. Their line of work could break me. The fact that you couldn't reach, or help, or save every child would destroy me.

"What's your name, honey?" I asked the little girl.

She was too weak to answer. Her mother handed me a laminated piece of paper, the girl's medical card. The mother's name was Prudence. The daughter's name was Mercy. It was not unusual apparently for little girls on the island to be given the names of virtues.

I reached into my pocket and pulled out all the money I had with me, which was about two hundred and fifty American dollars. I bent down and discreetly squeezed it into the mother's hand as I returned the card to her.

In the car on the way back, I closed my eyes and tried not to see anything. At the residence, Callie's private secretary met me at the car to tell me that Callie and Greg were out on official business and would not return until late.

I went up to the suite and called my parents. They both got on the line and asked if I'd spent any more time with Mrs. Morrissete, and I told them that I'd not seen her since New Year's Eve. They asked again about Callie and if she was well.

"I'll fill you in on everything when I get back," I told them.

I checked in with my editor, looked at the magazine site, read a couple of the new pieces that had just gone live, then I began writing another essay, this one about my visit to the island.

The next morning at breakfast, in the rooftop garden, on the rosewood table under the canopy, Callie told me that I could come with her and Greg to Finance and the Runner's wedding, which, as it turned out, was a last-minute decision. The wedding was taking place in two days.

"Are you sure I can come?" I asked.

"Of course," she said. Then looking down at the sun-drenched city and the blue-green ocean in the distance, she asked, "How did things go with your tour yesterday?"

"It was fine," I said. "I saw a lot."

"The guide is available again today," she said.

"I'm going to stay in and do some work," I said.

I thought she would scold me for working on what was supposed to be a vacation, but she didn't. "I've been reading your work for a while," she said instead. "I googled your name two years ago, and this website popped up, and I've been reading you there since. I wasn't sure you'd even remember me until I read what you wrote about me a few months ago."

"I hope it was okay that I did write about you," I said.

She reached for a large leather purse, which was dangling off the back of her chair. She placed the purse on her lap and out of it pulled a round pink velvet box, capped with a lilac bow. I knew the box well. I had given it to her when we were seven years old. Inside were the five rolls of taffeta, chiffon, brocade, damask, and gingham, multicolored ribbons I had gifted her. They were still neatly stored in their individual velvet-lined compartments, still coiled around their plastic spools, as though they had never been touched.

The next afternoon, she took me to see her father's ashes at the Charles Morrissete National Museum complex. On the walls of the cavernous lobby was a series of giant photographs, similarly posed official portraits, of a thin, dark, high-cheekboned man, who seemed to have only worn hip-length Nehru-jacketed suits. Callie looked a lot more like him than she did her mother, whom I couldn't imagine with such erect posture and with such a gleam in her eyes in front of a camera.

In an alcove facing the photographs was a silver urn, a shiny cube encased behind layers of shatterproof glass. Engraved on the wall on top of the urn, in giant calligraphy letters, was the phrase FATHER OF THE NATION AND MARTYR FOR ITS CAUSE. On the urn was also Charles Morrissete's name and the dates of his birth and death, which were thirty-nine years and three months apart.

"I know it's crazy," Callie said, "but I spent years and years wishing we'd all died together that day, Mum, him, and me."

I put my arms around her shoulders because that's all I could think to do.

"Then I kept hoping he was in hiding somewhere just like we were hiding in Brooklyn," she said.

I looked around and realized that there was no one nearby, no museum heads, even no security people. The place had been emptied for us.

"My mum suffered a lot because of me," she added. "That's why I'm not having any kids. Greg wants them, but I don't ever want to have them." She cocked her head to one side and folded her arms across her chest. "I don't ever want to have them," she said. "I'm going to have to tell him soon."

Finance and the Runner's wedding was out in the countryside, on the coast, in a small fishing village called Maafa. There were no hotels in Maafa, only fishing huts, gatehouses, cottages, and one or two villas, like the hillside mansion where I was staying with Callie and Greg and the rest of the wedding party.

At sunset, we all gathered on the horseshoe-shaped beach, between the rolling dunes and sea-grape-lined promenade, framed by towering limestone cliffs rising out of the turquoise water. The Runner's and Finance's parents were there along with a total of twenty siblings, aunts and uncles, and nieces and nephews. Everyone, except the bride and groom, who wore a simple silk dress and a tux, had on running clothes, which thankfully Callie had also provided for me.

The ceremony was held inside a sunken part of the beach, an oculus accessed through steps carved into the rose-pink beach rock. Greg was both the officiate and the best man. As I stood there listening to Finance and the Runner recite their very traditional vows, I could not keep my eyes off Callie. She was trying to look attentive, but instead she looked preoccupied and lost, a bit like she did when I first met her in Brooklyn. Minus the tears.

The wedding dinner was held in the villa where we were staying. We ate at a long table by an infinity pool overlooking the beach. I sat between Callie and one of the Runner's uncles, who spent the entire time lecturing Greg about everything from cricket and soccer to the International Monetary Fund and the World Bank. Thankfully, there was a sky full of stars to gaze at anytime one of us rolled our eyes.

After dinner, a wall of flames rose on the beach. It was time for the wedding bonfire, which according to Callie was a timeless tradition on the island.

"If the woman started having any regrets at this point, she'd just throw herself into the fire," Callie joked as the others got up from the table and started for the beach. Greg held out a hand to her, but she motioned for him to follow the others.

"You okay?" he asked.

She nodded, and he reluctantly walked away.

She leaned back in her chair and glanced up at the stars. When it looked like she wasn't going, I stayed behind to keep her company.

"I thought they'd have a huge wedding," I said.

"It's hard to plan one of those in two days," she said, smiling at last. "Besides, I think they've always wanted it funny and sweet."

A round of lightning sparked across the water,

far beyond the beach. Callie leaned forward to have a look at where it was coming from, but no thunder followed. There was no sign of a moon, either, which made both the lightning and the stars seem much more dazzling.

"Did you ever think of running for prime minister yourself?" I asked Callie, once the lightning stopped.

I remembered seeing an online interview, which was taped at one of the island's television stations, where she was asked that same question soon after her husband became prime minister. She'd seemed annoyed by it, sighing loudly, clenching her jaw, then fidgeting in her chair.

"Given what happened to my father, you surely could see why that job would personally have little appeal for me," she'd said.

"Right now, I'd rather be known as the rising man's wife than the late and great man's daughter," she told me by the pool that night.

"Are these your only choices?" I asked.

"Maybe they're the only ones I'm allowing myself," she said.

"What about your mother? What does she think about that?" I asked.

"You have no idea how much my mother has sacrificed," she snapped, jerking her head toward me. But her anger seemed aimed not necessarily at me, or at least not entirely.

We watched the animated silhouettes of the bride and groom and the wedding guests around the bonfire. From where we were sitting, Finance and the Runner looked like their two heads were shared by one body, in spite of the contrast in their black and white clothes. The wind carried their laughter to us, along with the voice of a female family member recalling how Finance and the Runner had met at a party at her house and how they'd broken up for a time when the Runner was competing abroad, then had gotten back together again.

"After my father was assassinated, everyone left us behind," Callie said, drowning out the family member's voice. "They got on their chartered planes and they left us behind."

"Why did they leave you behind?" I asked.

"Maybe fear. Maybe they thought we had other means of getting off the island. I don't know. All that matters is they left us behind."

Laughter rose again from the beach, above the sound of the waves; then from a slightly muffled distance, we heard her husband begin his bonfire toast. "May your love," he said, "always burn as bright as this fire tonight."

"Hear! Hear!" the others echoed.

"After she picked me up from school, we couldn't go back to the residence to get anything because we didn't know what was waiting there," Callie said. "So my mother went to the airport and begged to be allowed on a plane. We didn't even have money for the ticket."

"May your passion remain as hot as this fire tonight," Greg continued.

"The man who gave Mummy the tickets and the papers to get on the plane? He made her go to a back room with him before he gave them to her," Callie said. Her voice was clipped, her tone forceful. "I had to sit outside that room. I had to listen to him moan and moan and moan. At some point I opened the door. He was on top of her."

"May you walk through fire even hotter than this for each other," Greg said. "May your love remain an eternal flame."

"I was going to run in and shove him off," Callie said. "Off her, I mean. But Mummy saw me standing in the doorway. She motioned with one hand, just one hand, for me to wait. I did what she told me. I waited, because somehow I knew that, as soon as that was over, we'd be able to leave. There were all these rumors circulated about that moment, though. The story people told is that it was me. They say the man sat me on his lap and touched me everywhere while my mother watched. They said that was the price for getting on the plane."

The bonfire began to fizzle on the beach, the flames dimming. Suddenly I felt as though I were standing on a vast fault line, one between her and everyone else at that wedding. The difference between her and them was as stark as the gulf between those who'd escaped a catastrophe unscathed and others who'd been forever mutilated by it.

"You see," she told me. "No story is ever complete."

On Three Kings' Eve, my parents used to make me leave my shoes by my bedroom door for an angel to fill with rolls of hair ribbons while I slept. Before I went to sleep, they would tell me about a bad decision made by this angel, who they said looked like whoever is the most beautiful woman I know. This angel had been asked by the Three Kings to join them on their journey to bring gold, frankincense, and myrrh to the baby Jesus, and for some reason, she had turned them down. The angel regrets her decision to this day, my mother said, which is why she brings small presents to children on the eve of Three Kings' Day.

After we met, I wanted to be her angel and give Callie all my ribbons. Somehow I sensed that something about her needed to be bundled and held tight. Maybe she still needed to be bundled and held tight. Maybe that's why she'd held on to those ribbons for so long.

The next morning, I got up early to watch the sun rise over the beach in Maafa. At dawn, it looked as though clouds were pouring liquid gold into the surrounding headlands and cliffs, as well as into the sea. The flour-white sand turned the color of margarine. This, I realized, was one of the golden beaches Callie had been remembering when we were seven years old.

We left Finance and the Runner to their honeymoon in Maafa and returned to the residence just in time to catch the final moments of the island's archbishop's Three Kings' Day blessing, a favor which was apparently granted yearly at Mrs. Morrissete's request. Mrs. Morrissete was wearing a mauve Chanel jacket with a black bouclé skirt. She was clutching a rosary and kept her head lowered as she followed the archbishop throughout the first floor, while he sprinkled holy water and singsonged his blessings and prayers.

Out of the chaos of life, the archbishop said, would come peace over this house and all those who dwelled in it.

The archbishop walked over to Callie and Greg and drizzled their bowed heads with holy water as well. Then before leaving, he blessed Mrs. Morrissete, who blessed herself abundantly, crossing herself three times with her eyes squeezed tight.

Mrs. Morrissete had lunch prepared for the four of us. It was laid out beautifully on the rosewood table under the canopy on the roof. The lunch included a curried pork stew that I could barely eat because I kept looking at Mrs. Morrissete, meeting anew the now more apparent sorrow buried under her hesitant smile.

"How was the wedding?" she asked Callie.

"Beautiful," Callie said.

"Did anyone cry?" she asked Greg.

"Buckets," he said, though I hadn't noticed.

"I will never forget how kind your family was to us in New York," she told me. "Please be sure to give your parents my warmest regards."

Dessert was the galette des rois, the kings' cake that my parents also liked to have on Three Kings' Day. The tiny brown baby Jesus, nestled in the inner layers and linings for any lucky celebrant to find, ended up on my plate, and when I found it, I squealed like I always have, as though I were still a little girl.

Callie and Greg had an official Three Kings' Day parade to attend and were in a hurry to leave. I was going with them.

"Mummy, will you come?" Callie asked hesitantly as though she already knew what the answer would be.

Mrs. Morrissete shook her head no.

Callie lingered with her a bit after kissing her goodbye. Then as Greg and I were waiting by the elevator, Callie and her mother got up and walked over to the cabanas. They moved together to the glass railing, both clinging tightly to the top. As they took in the view of the old and new cities, and of the buildings and the sea, they turned their faces back and forth, their gaze lingering on some things, while quickly moving past others. It seemed to me, at that moment, that together they were watching over the entire island, as though they were its last sentinels.

Without Inspection

It took Arnold six and a half seconds to fall five hundred feet. During that time, an image of his son, Paris, flashed before his eyes: Paris, dressed in his red school-uniform shirt and khakis the day of his kindergarten graduation. That morning, Paris's mother, Darline, had skipped around the apartment changing dresses, as if she were the one graduating. Closing his eyes tightly as the hot wind he was plunging through battered his face, Arnold saw Paris at the classroom ceremony. He saw himself, too, standing next to Darline, who had finally chosen a billowing sapphire-colored satin dress. He was in the one black suit he wore to everything, to weddings and to funerals.

One reason not to own too many things was their crammed two-bedroom apartment, but the other, at least for him, had to do with never wanting to feel bound. To be attached to a few people was fine—to Paris and to Darline, who were as much a part of him as his blood was—but he never wanted to be tied to things, to clothes and shoes gathering dust in packed closets, to a fancy car that required hefty payments every month. No, it was simpler to be free. As free as this fall, which he had neither intended nor chosen, this dive that had resulted from his left foot slipping off the scaffold and his body sliding out of his either loosened or broken safety harness, as though a wrathful hand had pulled the straps off him, tipped him on his side, and tossed him into the air. Then his body, attempting to regain some control, had corrected the angle at which he had begun falling, so that he was now plummeting headfirst toward the ground, which was not yet concrete but dirt and soil, from which weeds, bushes, and flowers had been plucked to make way for a forty-eight-story hotel.

He was still falling, faster by the second. The wind felt increasingly resistant, each gust a hard blue veil to pierce through, even as the ground rose to meet him. His body veered farther left, and directly below him was an open cement-mixer chute, attached to a truck, the kind that had always looked like a spaceship to him.

He'd been looking down at the cement truck a few hours earlier as he sat on the scaffold platform eating his breakfast. Darline liked him to eat at home with her and Paris, but he was always in too much of a hurry to do it, except on the rare Saturdays and Sundays when neither of them had to work. During the week, he drove her to the Haitian restaurant where she was a cook, then he dropped Paris off at school. By the time he got to the construction site, he had just a couple of minutes to buy a guava pastry and a cup of coffee from the Lopez brothers' food truck.

What enterprising guys the Lopez brothers were. Only five years earlier, they'd arrived from Cojímar on a raft made from a refitted 1950s Chevy, and look at them now. The Lopez brothers' raft story, which he'd once heard them tell to another Cuban while he was waiting for his breakfast, had reminded him of his own landing, which was oh so different from theirs.

Darline had been the only person sitting on the beach in the predawn light the morning that he, nine other men, and four women were ditched in the middle of the sea and told by the captain to swim ashore. The sea was relatively calm that morning. As Arnold got closer to the beach, he also noticed the towering buildings, the tall glass edifices he'd always heard about.

All four women had drowned. They could not swim. Their bodies might eventually wash up on the beach, just as his did, except that he was still alive. Some of the men who had been on the boat with him were alive, too. They lay on the beach and tried to convince themselves, by digging their heels and toes into the sand, that they were no longer moving. He, on the other hand, just sat there looking at her. He did not want to walk over to her and frighten her away. He stank, and he was certain that the patchy beard he'd grown on the trip made him look menacing. She was staring back at him. Then he heard the sirens and he began pleading.

"Ede m"—help me—he mouthed. He did not want to be detained or returned. He wanted to stay. He **needed** to stay, and he was hoping to stay with her. She could have been anybody— whoever happened to be on the beach that morning and was willing to help him. But he was happy that it was her. Somehow, it felt as though they had a rendezvous, planned by someone neither of them knew.

The sirens jolted her and she got up and came over and took his arm, so that if the police did arrive as they were walking away together they might both be arrested or both be ignored, but whatever happened to one would surely happen to the other—because to anyone who was looking at them they appeared to be a couple, one of whom was soaking wet.

As they walked toward the parking lot, leaving the other men, still dazed and baffled, behind them, he heard a few of them shout out to her, but she did not look back. He followed her lead and didn't look back, either, even as some of them called his name.

One of the men yelled, "Your wife was waiting here for you, huh?"

Another, "Please don't leave us here."

Two of them tried to follow, but quickly gave up. Darline was walking too fast, and the men were tired. He, too, would have been trailing behind if she were not supporting him. She leaned in and said quietly, "An n ale, an n ale"— let's go—and sped up.

Her small white car was covered with dents

and scratches. He forgot that he was wet until she passed him the towel she'd been sitting on at the beach. He shook the sand off it before placing it on the front passenger seat.

"If you'd stayed, they would have taken you to Krome," she said.

He had no idea what or where Krome was.

"It's a prison for people like us," she said.

Us? What did she mean by "us"? Was this her way of telling him that she'd also come by boat? Had she been imprisoned in this place, Krome?

He wanted to ask her a dozen questions. He wanted to know why she had chosen him. Why rescue him and not the others? At least three more could have fit into the back seat of her car. But, more than curious, he was thirsty. So very thirsty.

Just as he was now, as he was falling.

He'd learned, while at sea, that time can stretch endlessly and that wind and air can suck you dry, forcing you to see what is not there. They had run out of clean water halfway through the trip from Port-de-Paix, on the northern coast of Haiti, and had had to drink seawater or their own urine. A trip that was supposed to take at most two days had actually taken four, because the captain kept changing course and once even changed speedboats to avoid run-ins with the US Coast Guard.

Before he could ask for water, she reached into the back seat and handed him a bottle from a pack of more than a dozen. If the police hadn't arrived, with their helicopters, cruisers, ambulances, and dogs, he might have taken some of that water to the people he'd left behind on the beach.

The police dogs he heard barking, she told him, were cadaver dogs. They were released on the beach to find corpses that might be hidden from view, because for every person who made it to shore maybe five others died. Why hadn't he dived back into the sea to rescue the others? Or at least dragged some of the corpses out? His own hunger and thirst, the weakness in his legs, had made him fear drowning if he went in again; his fear of being caught had made him crazy, or selfish.

He drank the water so fast it nearly choked him. She took the empty bottle and handed him another full one. He drank that, too.

"Where should I take you?" she asked him.

This was a service she provided, he realized. She was a volunteer chauffeur for boat people. Later, she would tell him that she'd done this for seventeen others, including women and children.

He now felt doubly sorry for the people he'd left behind, men and women he'd barely known when they embarked in Port-de-Paix, but with whom he'd grown familiar during the journey as they'd watched one another become both homesick and seasick, shrinking to sunburned skin and protruding bones. These other survivors would now have to confront their grief **and** the immigration police. Most, if not all, of them would be sent back. She had saved him from that.

"Ou grangou?" she asked him, once the water she gave him had diluted all the salt water in his stomach.

Before he could answer, she pulled over into a fast-food drive-through and ordered him two bags of food. Although it was the first food he had eaten in this country, he would never again enjoy breakfast burritos. He ate six of them, and then he threw up in the restroom of the fast-food place.

After he had cleaned himself up, they sat in her car in the parking lot, trying to figure out what to do next.

"I never take anyone to my home with me," she told him.

He hoped that this meant she was making an exception, because, now that he had eaten and was no longer thirsty, he looked her over carefully and found her body, which was both long and shapely, as pleasing as her face.

"There's a shelter . . ." She started driving again without finishing her sentence.

She took him to a church shelter, where he met some men like him, men who'd come on boats from Haiti, the Bahamas, and Cuba. He'd learned Spanish from the Dominicans he'd worked for as a stock boy on the border and picked up some turns of phrase and idioms from the shelter Cubans, who eventually helped him get the job on the construction site.

A few days after she left him at the shelter, he was playing dominoes with his new friends, while also watching a television perched against a back wall in the recreation room, when he saw a news story about a boat that had capsized in the waters near Turks and Caicos. Twelve bodies had been found: seven men, five women. Ten more were still missing.

He thought he would never see her again, but

she came by the shelter soon after he started working. They went out into the yard, where there was a set of rusty swings. The swings reminded him that children could also stay at this shelter, but, thankfully, there were none there now. Across from the swings was a basketball court, with a mural of adults and children playing in a tropical forest filled with coconut palms. They stood together by the swings.

"I have a son," she told him. "His father died at sea."

For a moment, he thought that she and the boy's father had been separated before this man died in the sea. But as her eyes filled with tears, he realized that she had been at sea with him. And that she had watched him drown the way those who'd come with Arnold had drowned.

"How did you make it?" he asked her.

"I had to pull our son out of the water," she said.

"What's your son's name?" he asked.

"Paris," she said, and, before he could respond, she added, "It was his father's dream to go there one day."

He then imagined the boy's father, a young man like himself, not just fleeing misery but answering the siren call of a distant city, where he felt he belonged. Arnold had been imagining a life in Miami since he was a boy. Many people he knew in Port-de-Paix had gone to the Bahamas by boat, and a few had moved from there to Miami. He'd felt as urgent a longing for Miami as Paris's father must have felt for the French capital.

What he had not foreseen about Miami, though, was the plethora of stories like his. He had also not realized that there would be homeless families sleeping under a bridge a few feet from the luxury hotel that he was helping to erect. The poor dead children he heard about in the news were also a shock to him, the ones who were randomly gunned down by the police or by one another, in schools, in their homes, while walking in the street, or playing in city parks.

It started drizzling in the yard with the swings. He thought that Darline would run inside and was ready to follow her, but she didn't move.

"Where's your son now?" he asked.

"I have a friend from work who has a boy like him, and she sometimes watches him for me. We take turns."

By "a boy like him," did she mean a fatherless boy, a sea-orphaned boy? Or did her child suffer from some type of infirmity?

"Is he sick?" he asked.

"He was the first one to fall in the water," she said. "It may have done something to his head."

She was laying out all her life's complications for him to consider. She was telling him that he could either go or stay. He wanted to stay.

She squeezed her body into a swing and tried to force it to move. He listened as the metal chains squeaked above her. She pushed herself back and forth a few times, then dug her shoes into the dirt to stop. When her feet were firmly on the ground, he leaned over and kissed her.

They went inside, and he asked her to wait in the dim, narrow hallway while he went to the room he shared with three other men and made her son a paper airplane. This was the only kind of toy he'd had when he was a boy. Whenever he found pieces of paper in the trash or on the ground, he'd make himself a paper airplane. Eventually, he had become an expert at it. The first paper airplane he made for Paris was plain white and unadorned, but it had long, narrow wings so it could fly far.

She had a habit of making lists in a small

notebook. Lists of things she needed to do for the day, lists of the people she'd taken to shelters from the beach, even though she hadn't gone there since rescuing him. The Coast Guard had become more vigilant, and the landings had decreased.

One day, she read him something from the notebook. His name was the only one on a list she titled "People from the Beach I Have Kissed."

He took the opportunity to ask her why she'd kept going back to that beach after her husband had drowned there.

She always called for help for those who were drowning, she said, just as she had the day Arnold arrived. She never jumped into the water to save anyone, because she didn't think she'd be able to stay afloat. Besides, a desperate person can use your head as a step stool to climb out of the waves, and she had her son to think about. She kept coming back to the beach because it was her husband's burial place, and her own. The person she'd been when the three of them, she and her husband and her son, had gotten on that boat and left Haiti—that person was also lost at sea.

. . .

This landing was even more abrupt than his last one. His free fall ended as his body slammed into the drum of the cement mixer. He was being tossed inside a dark blender full of grout. Every few seconds, his face would emerge from under the wet, pounded sand and pebbles, and he would keep his mouth closed, trying to force air out through his nose and push away the grainy mix that his body was trying to inhale.

He pretended that he was swimming and tried to flutter kick, just as he had when the speed-boat stopped in the middle of the ocean and he was told to swim ashore. He attempted arm strokes, but couldn't move either his arms or his legs. Still, his body was in constant motion, because the mixer continued to turn. He reached for the shaft, what in a more stable space, in a house or a temple or some other holy place, you might call a poto mitan, a middle pillar. He used what was left of his strength to propel his body toward the shaft and wrap his hands around it. He was able to hold on only briefly before he was pulled in another direction.

He felt lighter now, even lighter than he had when falling. His bones were melting, his blood evaporating, and he was now like parchment or something porous—tulle, or the white eyelet lace Darline adored. He had not been paying attention to the alternating hum and jangle of the mixer. He hadn't noticed that there were streaks of blood polluting the cement, or that he was feeling no pain. Then the mixer stopped spinning, and he heard the stillness, which was soon replaced by screams and grunts and "Oh, my God." Then he heard the sirens, which took him back to the beach, to the gray sand and Darline's sable face, her azure jogging suit, Paris's red shirt, and his own orange-and-green-speckled vomit at the fast-food place.

From where he was lying inside the cement mixer, he saw an airplane cut across the clear blue sky. And that was when he realized that he was dying, and that his dying offered him a kind of freedom he'd never had before. Whatever he thought about he could see in front of him. Whatever he wanted he could have, except what he wanted most of all, which was not to die. He had wished for something with wings to pluck him out of the cement mixer, and there it was up in the sky now, in the shape of an airplane. He and Darline had been putting money away to take Paris on an airplane. It was either a trip or a ring, and they were essentially already married, Darline had told him. Paris was their ring.

They loved each other and they loved him. He was their son.

He wanted to see Darline and Paris again. If only one last time. He wanted to see their faces. He wanted to hold their hands. He wanted to kiss them in the different ways he often had, her on the lips and him on top of his head, where his fontanel would be if he were still a baby.

The plane was slipping out of view, and he heard himself whisper, "Rete la, wait, quédate." He meant to tell the airplane to stay, or Darline and Paris to stay in his mind, but the fat pink face of his foreman was blocking the sky, and he heard the usually gruff man say, "Don't worry, Fernandez. I'm not going anywhere. Help is on the way, bud."

Oh, yes, the papers he'd used to get the job said that he was Ernesto Fernandez from Santiago de Cuba. No one on the site, not even the other Haitians, knew his real name. They didn't believe he was "Cuban Cuban," as they'd said, but since he spoke some Spanish, they thought he'd spent some time there and had taken the name.

He did not know how long this half consciousness would last, his being able to think and remember, so he wanted to keep pushing, to see how far he could take it. What if he made himself float out of the cement mixer? What if he traveled through the city and visited the only two people he loved? He wanted them to see him or, if they could not see him, sense him. He wasn't sure how this would work. They would feel a hot wind or a cold breeze. Something near them could move. A picture frame might slip, a drinking glass shatter. Might they notice his shadow out of the corner of their eye, sniff for his pungent after-work smell, or hear his favorite song? Would their palms itch? Would they feel the flutter of his kisses? Or would he appear in their dreams?

Paris might be more susceptible to receiving signs from him. The boy was already "touched." His mind had been partly lost somewhere between the sea and the beach.

Arnold felt the time growing shorter, so he would not be going all the way back to his childhood in Port-de-Paix. It was a time he'd been trying to forget anyway. He had never met his parents, never knew who they were. He had been raised as a child servant in a household, given away by whoever had brought him into the world. He knew only that he shared neither blood nor a surname with the woman in whose house he grew up. Nor did he have any biological link to her two sons, whose clothes he washed and ironed, whom he walked to school and cooked for, even though they were a few years older than him. Maybe his parents were dead. The woman who raised him had never mentioned them, except to say, whenever he messed up her food or didn't clean her house properly, that he was worthless and didn't deserve to have parents.

He had escaped her and her sons as soon as he could, moving to the border, where he slept in a warehouse from which he hauled bags of flour, sugar, and rice to Haitian vendors and merchants. It was one of those merchants who had told him about a boat leaving for Miami. Her brother was the captain, she said. He gave her all the money he'd been saving up so that he could go back and show his cruel owner and her sons that he'd made something of himself.

After he moved in with Darline, he learned, when she took him to a free immigration clinic in North Miami, that she was still waiting for her papers. She had just completed her baccalaureate in Haiti when she became pregnant with Paris. Paris's father had been her classmate in Latibonit, and they shared, as she put it, an impractical love. She loved her family. She loved her country. She wanted to stay in Latibonit. She wanted to grow old and die there. She and Paris's father had sufficient resources from their families to get by. But when Paris's father told her that he was leaving for Miami on a boat, there was no question of her and Paris staying behind.

"It was crazy," she told Arnold. "I thought I couldn't live without him. I thought I'd stop breathing if he wasn't near me. Especially after we'd made this baby together."

When they got to Miami, only she and Paris made it out of the water. Her husband's body was never found. After a short hospital stay, they were sent to a women's shelter. The lawyer at the immigration clinic called it "humanitarian parole." The same lawyer told Arnold that he had entered the country "without inspection." That is, he had not gone before any immigration official the day he arrived in the United States, which meant that, technically, he wasn't even here.

I want to see Darline, Arnold told himself. He now had a better sense of how this might work. What he didn't know was whether or not there were limits to the wishes he could be granted.

Suddenly he was standing in the kitchen of the restaurant in Little Haiti where Darline worked. The room was small and steamy, the walls grease-stained. She was cooking a large pot of cornmeal with red beans. Next to that was an equally large pot of stewed codfish. He had been in the kitchen so many times that perhaps he was just remembering it. She was perspiring so much that it was hard for him to imagine that she could last a whole day there. She took a swig from a bottle of water, then raised the lid of a pot of boiling plantains. As she worked, she hummed a song that he began to hum, too. Maybe she would feel him humming along. Perhaps she would even hear him.

"Latibonit O" was the only song he had ever heard her sing. She sang it so often that she didn't realize she was doing it. She sang it when she was happy, when she was worried, when she was sad. She started to sing it now.

Latibonit o, yo voye pale m, yo di m Sole malad . . .

The song, he believed, was about a sick sun looming over the town where she was born. He sang along to the part where the sun becomes bedridden, then dies and is buried. The song had always been, in his mind, a solemn farewell to the golden hour before sunset. He didn't know what the sunsets over Latibonit looked like, but Port-de-Paix had the most beautiful sunsets, muted just enough not to blind you when you looked directly at the horizon. He now missed how time had seemed to stand still at those moments, if only for the duration of a single post-dusk breath.

He sang along as loudly as he could, but he could not produce audible sounds. This, he discovered, was one of his limitations. He heard a buzz coming from Darline's apron, a familiar vibration. It was her cell phone.

Whatever she heard after she said hello annoyed her. She dropped the wooden spoon she was using to gently move the boiling plantains around. She sucked her teeth in exasperation, and it sounded as though she were whistling through them.

Her friend Oula came in with several orders. Darline looked so distracted that Oula asked, "Sa k genyen, Darline?"

"It's Paris," she said.

"That teacher bothering you about him again?" True to her name, Oula was always there when Darline needed her. Oula also had a son who teachers thought was slow.

He did not know how long he had, so he said Paris's name and hoped that it would be interpreted as a desire to see the boy.

It was morning recess at Paris's school. Paris was sitting alone in a corner between two bookshelves, making boats out of some sheets of paper that the teacher had given him. Arnold and Paris had gone from making paper airplanes together to making boats. This activity helped Paris focus, but it also helped Arnold. The boats reminded him that he had survived the sea.

The other children were eating their snacks and chasing one another around the classroom as the teacher threatened them with time-outs and other forms of deprivation. Paris did not even look up to observe the commotion. The principal of the school had wanted to put Paris in a special class, but Darline had refused. He was not disruptive, just overly engrossed in certain things, Darline had told the principal and anyone else who wanted to label her son anything but shy.

Arnold knew childhood stigma too well not to agree with Darline. Paris's teachers could not understand what the boy had been through. They did not know that his father had disappeared just a few feet from him. Paris seemed to be in perpetual mourning, like his mother.

Paris had called Arnold "Papa" the first time they met. Darline had arranged for them to have a meal together after hours at the restaurant where she worked. Paris had said nothing during the meal, but, as Arnold was leaving, he asked, "Are you my papa?"

"I could be," Arnold said.

Darline smiled, and Paris jumped into his arms. Both seemed to take his answer as a gift he was offering. Suddenly his life meant something. He became a father.

In Paris's classroom, Arnold crouched down next to the boy, in the narrow space between the bookshelves. He tried to wrap his arms around Paris but could no more feel the boy's body than the boy could feel his.

He moved his head close to Paris's and pressed his mouth against the boy's right ear and shouted so that he might possibly be heard: "Paris, my son, one day you will go to the other Paris. You will have a family and you will fly in a real airplane."

He looked for a sign that the boy had heard him or even felt his presence, but he saw none.

Paris was now on his eighth paper boat. He was folding lengthwise, then at the corners. There was always a moment in their boat making when Arnold thought that Paris might be content to stop at what looked like a hat, but then he continued until a stern or a hull emerged.

"Goodbye, Paris," he shouted into the boy's ear. "Please love your mother forever."

Then he smiled as the boy reached up and flicked the ear he was shouting into, as though something small, like a buzzing mosquito, had grazed him there.

Paris disappeared. Or maybe it was Arnold who'd disappeared.

He was back at the construction site. Not wounded but whole, just as he had been when he left home that morning. He was still wearing his bright orange overalls and matching hard hat. Was time playing with him, or was he playing with time? Was he skirting the yellow police tape in the present or in the past?

The site was closed down, and many of the men he worked with were milling around, leaning over the tape to better see the photographers who were taking pictures of the cement mixer. News trucks with extended antennas were lined up across the street, and reporters were interviewing some of his coworkers and a few passersby, many of whom claimed that they had seen him fall. His body had flailed wildly at first, they said, then plunged directly into the cement chute.

The construction company and the developer had already issued a statement, which was read by many of the reporters for their midday broadcasts: "We are deeply saddened by the tragic death of Ernesto Fernandez. We offer our condolences to his family, his friends, and his coworkers. We are working with state and federal investigators to find out how this unfortunate accident took place and to prevent further incidents of this nature in the future."

There were cell-phone videos of him falling, taken from different angles. Some people had filmed him from the ground. Others had recorded him from their terraces and balconies. He looked, in the quickly assembled collage of these recordings, not like a person but like a large object plummeting. He was moving too fast to be identifiable as a human being when the footage wasn't in slow motion.

The lightness returned. That airless sensation of his body evaporating. Darline and Paris were fading, too. They were becoming distant longings, silhouettes, shadows fading on the ground.

There are loves that outlive lovers. Some version of these words had been his prayer as he fell. Darline would now have two of those. He would also have two: Darline and Paris. He would keep trying to look for them. He would continue to hum along with Darline's song, and keep whispering in Paris's ear. He would also try to guide Darline back to the beach, to look for others like him.

Acknowledgments

I am deeply grateful to Kathy Neustadt, Nancy Neustadt Barcelo, Susan Neustadt Schwartz, the University of Oklahoma, Daniel Simon, and **World Literature Today** for the 2018 Neustadt International Prize for Literature, and to the Ford Foundation for the 2018 Art of Change Fellowship. Both honors have not only placed me in extraordinary company but have led to some wonderful creations and exquisite collaborations. Thank you, Elizabeth Alexander and Achy Obejas, for modeling writerly advocacy so beautifully. I am extremely grateful to Nicole Aragi, Charles Rowell, and Deborah Treisman, who are often the first readers of my short stories. Thank you, Robin Desser, for traveling this road with me for so long. And thanks to my family—Bob, Kelly, Karl, Fedo, Mira, Leila, Madame Boyer, and the whole Danticat and Boyer gang—for everything I can and cannot name.

"Being born is the first exile . . ." is from Cindy Jiménez-Vera's poem "COULD YOU TALK TO US ABOUT YOUR COUNTRY'S HISTORICAL MEMORY?," which can be found in **I'll Trade You This Island: Selected Poems,** translated by Guillermo Rebollo-Gil (Ediciones Aguadulce, Biblioteca Desembocadura, 2018). "We love because it's the only true adventure . . ." is from Nikki Giovanni's poem "Love: Is a Human Condition," which can be found in **The Collected Poetry of Nikki Giovanni: 1968–1998** (Harper Perennial Modern Classics, January 2007). The lyrics to "Shall We Gather at the River?" are from the hymn "At the River," written by Robert Lowry in 1864. Nina Simone's "Take Me to the Water" is referring to a version of this song recorded live at Morehouse College in Atlanta in June 1969. Charles Mingus's "Haitian Fight Song" is from his album **The Clown,** recorded in 1957. "Latibonit O" is a well-known Haitian folk song that invokes the Artibonite region—Latibonit—in the north of Haiti. The way the lyrics are translated is based on whether one believes that the "Sole" being referred to in the song is the sun (normally spelled "solèy") or a person named Sole. If one believes that it is the sun, as my character does, the first verse referred to in the story "Without Inspection" can be translated thus:

**O Artibonite, they sent me word
that the sun is sick.
When I arrive, I find the sun in bed.
When I arrive, I find the sun is dead.
Regretfully, I must bury the sun.
It pains me so to bury the sun.**

Credits

These stories first appeared, in different forms, in the following publications: "Dosas" as "Elsie" (Winter 2006) and "In the Old Days" (Spring 2012) in **Callaloo;** "The Gift" as "Bastille Day" (June 2011) in **The Caribbean Writer;** "Hot-Air Balloons" (Spring 2011) in **Granta** magazine; "The Port-au-Prince Marriage Special" (October 2013) in **Ms.** magazine; "Sunrise, Sunset" (July 2017) and "Without Inspection" (May 2018) in **The New Yorker;** and an excerpt from "Seven Stories" as "Quality Control" (Fall 2014) in **The Washington Post Magazine.**

A NOTE ABOUT THE AUTHOR

Edwidge Danticat is the author of numerous books, including **The Art of Death,** a National Book Critics Circle finalist; **Claire of the Sea Light,** a **New York Times** Notable Book; **Brother, I'm Dying,** a National Book Critics Circle Award winner and National Book Award finalist; **The Dew Breaker,** a PEN/Faulkner Award finalist and winner of the inaugural Story Prize; **The Farming of Bones,** an American Book Award winner; **Breath, Eyes, Memory,** an Oprah's Book Club selection; and **Krik? Krak!,** also a National Book Award finalist. A 2018 Neustadt International Prize for Literature winner and the recipient of a MacArthur "Genius Grant," she has been published in **The New Yorker, The New York Times, Harper's Magazine,** and elsewhere.